THE LEOPARD OF TRYCE

The way up is the way down

BY

P. S. NAUMANN, S.J.

COVER DESIGN AND ILLUSTRATION BY
JAY MONTGOMERY

Copyright © 2013 P. S. Naumann, S.J. *author of Crispin and the Great Tree*

All rights reserved.

ISBN 10: 1480085685

EAN 13: 9781480085688

DEDICATION

For the greater glory of God certainly,
and for my family
extended both vertically
and horizontally.

Also by P. S. Naumann, S.J.
Crispin and the Great Tree

NOTE

The Atlantic Archipelago,
fictitious setting of these books,
consists of seven islands ruled by Nine Houses or families.
The Archipelago lies in the mid-Atlantic
somewhere not too far south of Iceland.
Like the Althing of Iceland,
the Archipelago has an Allgathering once a year.
At this, the heads of the Nine Houses, the bishops and the abbots
meet to settle juridical matters and, rarely,
to make a law binding on all.
In alphabetical order the Nine Houses are as follows:
Falconstryke, Laggenhorst, Montalban, Rintoul, Skarpingdin,
Southlocke, Trefoil, Tryce, and Whithorn.

The Atlantic Archipelago disappears
when you close the covers of this book.

ONE

THE ARCHDUKE'S CASTLE

"It's night! I didn't think it would be night!"

"Where are we?"

"Wait till I collapse the umbrella." This umbrella had just brought the two boys instantaneously from the lawn of Longshanks Hall in 1930 to the battlements of this castle in 1580. "Ah! We're on one of the towers."

"Thanks. I could see that."

"Shhhhhh. Don't make so much noise. There may be sentries or something."

A chill night wind blew over the towers of Tryceholdings Guard, the Archduke's castle. Crispin crawled towards the battlements, stood up slowly, and looked over. His eyes were still growing accustomed to the dark but shapes gradually became themselves and recognizable. Tarquin, his older brother, came and stood beside him.

"We're on the northeast corner," Crispin said in a whisper. "It's the Chapel Tower. Look, the whole castle is in front of us, the inner ward and then the outer ward beyond."

Just below them there was, indeed, a sentry, but he was tramping away from them down the wall walk, using his partisan as a walking staff rather than a weapon. He stopped, started again, then sneezed and wiped his nose on his sleeve. Occasionally he hawked up something and spat over the parapet or down into the ward, depending on which side was closer.

He doesn't want to be out here with his cold, thought Crispin. The sentry passed the tower at the corner of the inner ward and kept going.

"O K, which way to the Archduke?" asked Tarquin, who was spoiling for adventure, any adventure.

"He's probably in that room down there. See the lights shining into the garden. Here's the stairway down," and he opened a door onto a spiral staircase.

The two boys crept silently down the stone steps, keeping to the outside where there was wider footing. Crispin stopped. He pulled his brother's head down so that he could whisper in his ear.

"These steps were made deliberately uneven to throw off unfamiliar attackers, so be very careful."

"O K, O K, keep going."

They came to a door, closed, and kept going. The next door down was not closed, but invitingly ajar, though not enough to slide through. So Crispin handed the umbrella to Tarquin and put his face to the opening to see what he could see. What he saw was a narrow stone passage with a little light coming from around a corner at its end. And voices, he could hear voices, but just barely. *It must be the Leopard and some of his cronies*, he thought. He could feel Tarquin breathing down his neck, trying to see past him. He pushed ever so gently on the door. It swung open slightly, making no sound, and the two boys slid through.

Their sneakers made no noise on the stone floor as they crept down to the corner and cautiously looked around. The reason so little light shone into the passage was that hangings were drawn partially over the doorway at the end. The voices were louder but still muffled; nevertheless, Crispin recognized the harsh, metallic rasp of the voice of Axel, Archduke of Tryce. He had already been confronted by the so-called "Leopard of Tryce" on two memorable occasions, and now that sound made him wish he was back in the security and sunshine of the lawn he had just left. But his brother had already pushed ahead of him, and had an eye at the opening, at the same time being careful not to let the light shine on the rest of him.

"There are four men around a table." Tarquin turned back and whispered in his ear. "And two leopards."

"We knew there might be leopards. Let me take a look."

He put one eye to the opening and looked through. As he did this the leopards raised their heads as one and looked in his direction. Fortunately, the men were preoccupied by the map spread out in front of them. Yes, there was Archduke Axel at the head of the table. He wore a long dark red robe trimmed with fur at neck and sleeve-ends. The other three he did not recognize. They were wearing riding outfits and had thrown their long cloaks over the backs of chairs. These men were not the henchmen he had seen a month ago in the Forest of Harklinden. *Where are they?* he wondered.

"This is the road from Shipman's Brink to the abbey," the Archduke traced a line on the map. "It was built to transport large building stones brought by water. The road is perfectly plain, even at night, and broad enough to accommodate our troop, even four abreast."

"Great! Then that's the way we'll go," and the two others nodded agreement.

"No, no, no," said the Leopard. "There is neither bridge nor ferry at the Brink. Purposely never built, to discourage poachers from getting into the forest. So we cannot cross at that point. And we could not get through Shipman's Brink unseen or unheard."

"What then?"

"The only way is by the ford. That puts us across the river but further away from Longshanks Hall, as Chase is calling it, and the trail is narrow from the abbey through the forest. We can only go two by two," and he traced a different, twisting line across the map.

Crispin discovered that his brother had stretched out flat on the floor in the shadow of the hangings, but where he too could listen to what was being said.

"Is that a problem?" asked one of the men.

"The problem is here!" Axel struck the map with his finger, "with the Guardian of the Ford. He will never let us pass."

"But he's only one man!"

"And easily disposed of, one would think," said the Archduke with a grating chuckle, joined in by the other three.

As Crispin listened he began to realize that, encouraged by the Leopard of Tryce, they were plotting an attack on Longshanks Hall with fire and sword, to burn the place down and drive off the horses like rustlers. But when? And how many would there be? And . . .

"There remains one important detail," the Archduke was saying, "and that is passage through the forest itself. My brother Blaise, that grey wolf of an abbot, will never permit passage through his forest for such an escapade. And he would like nothing better than to turn me over to the law."

"But *you* are the law here."

"In the Tryceholdings, yes! But Longshanks Hall is not a part of the Holdings. However, lest you become too discouraged," he jangled a silver bell that stood holding down one corner of the map, "I think I have solved our problem before it even raises its ugly head." A man that Crispin recognized as one of the Leopard's henchmen, had come through the door at the other end of the room. "Fetch in the bishop," Axel directed.

The man nodded and kept on coming, heading directly for the door where the two boys were concealed. Tarquin leapt to his feet. They had not time to run back down the passage. They had not time to think. They had time only for instinct. They flattened themselves against the wall behind the hangings, one on either side of the door, where, fortunately, they stood in deep shadow. Through the door the henchman came, sweeping the hangings aside with both hands and letting in light. But the hangings fell back into place, returning the two boys to the dark.

"Milord, it's time!" the man cried in a hearty voice.

Moments later he returned with the bishop in tow. This time he stepped aside, held the curtains back on one side (his back almost brushed against Crispin), and let the bishop enter first. He was dressed in long, purple robes, fur-trimmed, and carried a leather portfolio clutched to his chest. A trim man in his early fifties but with face, nevertheless, looking drawn and pale. Crispin's throat clenched when he realized that the bishop had been in the chapel down the passage behind them all the time they were spying on the conspirators. The bishop looked neither to left nor right but passed unhappily into the lighted chamber. The henchman followed, letting the hangings drop behind him.

"Gentlemen, let me introduce Bishop Trycewinning, a distant cousin, my sole living relative. Apart, that is, from my brother, the Abbot Blaise. The bishop was happily forwarded to Tryceholdings by Rome to keep him out of trouble." The Archduke's voice was like iron under silk. "There is no need to kiss his ring. Sit down, Milord. Dorn, place a chair for the bishop."

There was the noise of a chair being dragged forward and the 'swatch' as the bishop dropped his portfolio onto the table.

"The bishop has been gracious enough to convince Rome, by the application of some pressure, that the abbey should be placed under a ban, the abbot and monks to be turned out, and the entire forest to be administered by me. You have the documents under the papal seal and all is satisfactory, I presume?"

"I have the document. Whether it is satisfactory or not depends . . ."

"I do not like that word *depends*. What could it possibly depend on?"

"There *are* conditions." The bishop's voice had a tremor in it.

"I like *that* word even less. How can there be conditions? There were to be no conditions." As the Archduke's anger rose, his voice became softer but more deliberate.

"May I ask what these conditions are?"

"That the abbey be forewarned before promulgation."

"Yeees."

"And that the ban be lifted . . ."

"Lifted!" The storm broke. The Leopard's two fists crashed down on the table as he sprang to his feet. At the same time his voice leapt into manic volume. "There was no talk of lifting; there will *be no* lifting!" It was a performance. From previous experience Crispin knew that it was a performance. Unfortunately the bishop did not.

". . . on the fulfillment of certain conditions . . ."

"That word again! Strike that word from your vocabulary!"

". . . to be set by you."

"Very clever. You are very clever, Bishop. Perhaps I have misjudged you all along." The Archduke's voice narrowed, as did his eyes. "I myself will announce the ban to the Abbot of Harklinden. Tomorrow. You, Bishop Trycewinning, will promulgate the ban publicly, in the cathedral, a week from that day. No doubt you have something for me to sign as future Administrator."

"I do."

"Leave it. I would like to look it over carefully."

"It must be signed in my presence."

"Ah. Of course. Excuse me, gentlemen, while I do my clerical chores." Both boys heard the scraping of chairs as the other three men moved away from the table, and then the scraping of their voices as they talked in low, harsh tones, drawing closer to the place of hiding where Crispin and Tarquin were holding their breaths.

But then the bell jangled, and the Archduke commanded, "Pen and ink." The voices retreated, the chairs scraped, and the voice of the bishop said, "Just there, your grace, in the blank space." In the silence a quill scratched. Crispin could shut his eyes and see the bold, black **Tryce** that the Archduke made. After that the bishop himself signed. Then the Leopard said, "I trust that your name will not prove prophetic. But then, I will see that it does not."

"Your grace?"

"Oh, never mind." With unquestionable authority, the Leopard continued, "By the time you reach the courtyard, you will have forgotten everyone you have seen here tonight "Indeed."

The bell jangled again. "Dorn, take Bishop Trycewinning down the outside stairway. I will see these gentlemen down to the Water Stairs, myself.

"Thank you, your grace," said the bishop, not without irony, "and good night."

While everyone's attention was directed towards the departing bishop, Crispin hooked Tarquin's arm with the umbrella handle and pulled him softly down the passage and into the round chapel that gave the tower its name.

"They don't have to come through here to get to the Water Stairs. That's down the same stairs we came down." Then they both strained to hear what the Leopard was saying to his confederates.

"Remember, if no one knows about this escapade, word cannot leak out to Longshanks or to the Ford. Therefore, we four shall swear an oath."

There was silence. Then they agreed. So the Leopard read the oath which so filled Crispin with dread that he felt his hair must be turning white and, too late, he clapped his hands over his ears.

"Blood, blood!" cried the Leopard, "Prick your thumbs and seal with blood next to your names."

"I cannot write," said a reluctant voice.

"Make your mark with the pen and with your blood and I will write your name for you. There. All is done. Now, my fellow conspirators, follow me down to the Water Stairs. Bring that torch, lest we go astray in the dark," and he laughed to himself. "It will be better if Chase Longshanks goes astray into the perpetual dark." Then all four laughed.

The torchlight flared in the passageway, the footsteps passed down the stairs with a faint ring of spurs. Quiet.

The two brothers had retreated into the depth of the chapel, where it was so dark that Crispin could see nothing of the wall painting he had seen only once before. But anyway, it was time to use the umbrella to return to Longshanks Hall.

TWO

THE COLONEL TELLS ALL

Crispin had already heard the story of Chase Longshanks from Colonel Falkrest, the current owner of Longshanks Hall. The boy, on his first remarkable quest, had arrived at the Hall at the time of the auction. The colonel had been auctioning-off everything he possibly could to pay off his racing debts and save the estate for his daughter, Sarah, and himself. The girl, just two years older than Crispin's seven, was confined to a wheelchair as the result of polio. She had made the boy promise to return once he had completed his quest. And he had kept that promise.

When he arrived, the lawns of Longshanks Hall looked ragged and uncut, except the front circle, which was still immaculately mowed. The slivery-green Pierce Arrow glided to a halt before the door. Crispin and Blight (who was twenty-one and doing the driving) got out. It was on that return visit that the colonel had told the Chase Longshanks story to Crispin and his older companion, Blight of Priorfields, who acted as the young boy's chauffeur, advisor, and friend.

Sarah had invited them to stay for lunch, in spite of the fact that she and her father were hard-pressed to make ends meet. The three were already at table having bowls of soup before Colonel Falkrest slid into his chair at the head of the table. "Of course I remember this young man. Crispin, isn't it?" He shook the boy's hand heartily. He smelt of leather and Bay Rum, with horse just vaguely somewhere underneath. "And . . . ?" he paused.

"Blight, sir."

"Ah yes. Blight. We only saw you from the other end of the Hall. You are, both of you, most welcome. What has the Silent Woman provided in that tureen?" The Silent Woman (Mrs. Converse, the cook), along with McGuiness (jack of all trades plus faithful family retainer), were the only two to remain in place after the auction.

McGuiness, at the sideboard, ladled out a bowl of soup and placed it on the plate in front of the Colonel, and provided him with a thick slice of bread, as he had the other three. Crispin was a little embarrassed because he seemed unable to keep his bread crumbs on his plate. Whenever he broke off a piece, the crumbs scattered across the tablecloth like children at the recess bell. Next, the tureen disappeared down the dumbwaiter. The boy had never seen one of these contraptions before, a two-tiered box that rose and fell as McGuiness operated the ropes. That rough-edged retainer stuck his head into the shaft and gave a shrill whistle between his teeth to let Mrs. Converse know that they were finished with the soup.

"We might have wanted seconds, Mac," Sarah said, as gently as possible, looking from Crispin to Blight.

"Sorry Miss, there are no seconds."

Crispin saw Sarah cock an eyebrow at her father but he was too polite to try to intercept the return glance. Instead, he asked about the Colonel's horse, "Is that Aladdin out there?" From where he sat he could just see a horse through the open windows. It was grazing on the other side of a white rail fence, the boundary of the gardens and lawns.

"That's my black beauty, poor lonely horse. What a ride he gave me this . . . well." He looked apologetically at his daughter in her wheelchair.

"It's all right, Dads. Tell me all you want; I love hearing about Aladdin even through I can't ride anymore. My black days are over, I hope, but I'll let you know if they come again. We were talking about how this place came to be called 'Longshanks' rather than 'Trycemeadows.' Can you tell us?" She nodded to McGuiness who served them small dishes of pineapple chunks and one cookie apiece.

"Trycemeadows! Haven't I told you that piece of ancient history before now? I certainly meant to."

The girl, who had begun keeping the financial records and was investigating the old ledgers, said, "No Dads, you never did, but all the oldest records, the rolled up parchment ones in Latin, are all "Trycemeadows."

"Well, let me see if I can reconstruct this episode as I heard it when I was about your age, Sarah. I'm afraid it's a racing story. Like almost every other Longshanks story." The girl nodded and smiled as though she had expected as much.

"It was the last Archduke, the one they called the 'Leopard of Tryce,' that lost Trycemeadows." Crispin glanced swiftly at Blight, whose eyebrow flicked, but he looked fixedly at Colonel Falkrest, who was gathering the threads of his story together.

"As a young man, Axel was the leader of a pack of wild followers, desperadoes, continually in trouble and continually vying with one another to see who could perform the most outrageous, daring feat. Or the most disruptive. The old Archduke made Trycemeadows over to Axel in the hope that the responsibility would steady him. And even if it didn't, it would get him out of Tryceholdings Guard. 'Out of sight, out of mind,' I suppose the old Archduke thought. The castle and the town had been in perpetual uproar because of Axel and his gang. Market days were especially trying, at least for the buyers and sellers. The plan didn't work. It just displaced the maelstrom from one county to the next. So, Trycemeadows became the . . . Mecca for every young ne'er-do-well in the entire Archipelago."

"Apes of idleness," Sarah interjected.

"Exactly. Where did you get *that* expression?"

"It's what Shakespeare calls them in a similar context. Dads, go on."

"There was drinking (plenty of that), and gambling, debauchery (whatever *that* means), and dabbling in the black arts. The style of living was very high — musicians in the gallery, fleets of cooks and bakers in the kitchens, and retainers to hustle dishes back and forth to the Hall or wherever they were called for, legions of grooms, horsemen, stablemen and boys — it was run like a royal establishment, but without the taxes to support it.

"Then one day a new young man showed up. He was very tall and rode a great red horse, also very tall. The young man introduced himself as Chase Longshanks. I'm not sure he was known as Longshanks (a name he could easily have shared with his horse) because he was particularly tall or because his horse was particularly tall. Both, I suspect. It wasn't long before Chase became a ringleader, second only to Axel. He rode harder, faster, and jumped higher obstacles than anyone with the possible exception of Axel himself.

"Well, naturally a rivalry developed, friendly at first but becoming more and more serious, and finally bitter. Chase drank very little; consequently he was always clear-headed when others were not. No doubt that explains much of his success at gambling. Because he always kept open house, Axel went into serious debt, mortgaged Trycemeadows, and went even deeper in.

"Now, I give you one guess. Who do you suppose was gathering up all of Axel's debts into his own hands? Crispin?"

"It could only be Chase Longshanks, I think."

"You are right, of course. How did you figure that?"

"Well, sir, he's the only other character in your story."

"Smart lad. So, Sarah and gentlemen, things went from bad to worse, as they generally have a way of doing. Axel could see the end overtaking him when he would lose everything and have to return empty-handed to his father, the Archduke. He tried one last desperate gamble. He challenged Chase to a race: if Axel won, all debts would be canceled; if Chase won . . . well, you know, Trycemeadows would be his, but all the debts as well. Not the most honest of bargains but honesty was not one of Axel's virtues, whatever the others might have been.

"Axel had a magnificent black hunter, Backlash by name, of which he was immensely proud. It was a nasty brute, they say, like its master, but with enormous endurance. Axel laid out the race-course in a great rough circle covering a large section of his lands. I have tried to figure out just how the course must have gone and have it down pretty well, I think, except for a wrinkle here and there. The land hasn't changed all that much from one century to another, but the wrinkles seem quite impossible to me on Aladdin. The walls are petty much the same, of course, but the hedges are a great deal higher and stream banks have shifted, in some cases considerably. Frankly, it was a course that I wouldn't want to have to race myself.

"The day before the race Chase walked the entire course – it took him most of the day – judging distances, heights of hedges and walls, footing on both sides of streams, steepness of inclines, leaving as little as possible to chance. He also looked for places of possible ambush. They say he slept in the stables the night before, to make sure nothing happened to his horse. Axel apparently spent his time plotting 'accidents' -- wagons that would unexpectedly block lanes and gateways, that sort of thing.

"Word of the race had spread faster than bad news. Everyone who could get here came, sometimes traveling for more than a day or two. So there were plenty of wagons, some drawn by oxen, some by horses. More than one of them had whole families and neighborhoods aboard. They pulled into every available nook and cranny along the course. How could anyone tell the inconvenient spectators from Axel's henchmen or, who knows, hench-women? On the other hand, Axel was not a popular landlord or neighbor.

Besides, Chase had not a few men of his own mixing with the crowds.

"The two racers mounted; the flag came down at the first stroke of noon in the Shanksmare steeple, and they were off! It was a race I would have loved to watch, every foot of it. It took two hours and seems to have been impossible to call until the very end. The last leg was from Shanksmare up what is now our front drive. You know how it rises and rises gently but steadily – incredible for a horse at the end of a race. Axel was ahead on Backlash coming up to the last rise. Then Chase simply took off. He had been saving his great red horse as carefully as he could, and won by over a length, coming down into the vale were this house still stands.

"Axel was enraged, but it made no difference. Everything had been carefully witnessed, and 'Trycemeadows' became 'Longshanks'. 'I'm not called 'Chase' because I come in second,' he said. And d'you know what?"

"No, Dads, tell us."

"Chase turned everybody out; sent them all packing. Axel left vowing terrible revenge; nevertheless, out went the apes of idleness, all of them, the musicians and all the upstairs and downstairs crew. He even sacked the stablemen, started all over again from scratch, very much as we are doing, Zascha," and he put a hand over his daughter's on the table.

"But what was the name of Chase's horse?" Crispin asked.

"Oh. Did I fail to mention that?" The Colonel's eyes sparkled. "It was Vortex."

THREE

A HORSE AND AN UMBRELLA

"But *I'm* learning to ride Vortex!" exclaimed Crispin, looking from one face to another around the table.

"You mean the Riverford horse?" asked Sarah in surprise. "I thought nobody could ride him except Riverford himself. I *am* impressed." (Fritz Riverford was Crispin's uncle and the current Guardian of the Ford.)

"Fritz may have put that story about so that nobody would ask," her father said.

"He's as gentle as cream pie; it's just that he's so big everyone keeps out of his way. But can he be in the same family as Chase's Vortex?" asked Crispin.

"Direct descendant," the Colonel declared, who knew the history of every thoroughbred in his own county and most of the thoroughbreds in the Archipelago.

"I'm glad you're learning to ride. Why didn't you tell me?" asked Sarah.

"He looks like a young trooper on Vortex, and rides like one too. You ought to see him go over the local hen houses," put in Blight with a twinkle in his eyes. "And becoming quite notorious in the neighborhood, I hear."

The boy blushed and said, ruefully, "Well, we don't do that anymore. Uncle Fritz sent me into the forest instead. There's nobody's chickens in there, nor cows either."

* * *

After his first riding lesson, Crispin had stayed with his uncle at Fritz Riverford's ancient inn, The Legendary Boar. The next few weeks he spent learning the different gaits and how to put Vortex through them, and learning to jump. First over the lowest bars, which his uncle gradually raised, and then over higher bars as he felt comfortable with them, then over the hedge in front of the inn, over the stream at Runnelstead, and finally an all-out steeplechase through neighboring pastures and fields. These gallops went on for the next few days. Local farmers and their wives were startled to look up and see the boy and horse tearing hell-bent-for-leather through their pastures or floating over their orchard walls or hen houses. The horse they knew; the boy was strange. "Who's that up on Vortex?" they asked one another. Then the telephone calls began.

"Crispin?"

"mmmph."

"I'm sorry, I should have known better than to start a question while your mouth was full."

The boy swallowed, everything at once.. "Yes, sir?"

"When you take Vortex out, do you stick to the bridle paths, or not?"

Awkward pause.

"Not."

"Yes, that's what I have been hearing on the telephone. Mrs. Reed tells me that she is still trying to pacify her hens, after she coaxed them down out of the trees and off the barnyard roofs. And Farmer

Landskip says much the same thing about his cows, that their milk has gone off." He paused. "Or maybe it was the other way around."

"Sir?"

It may have been Landskip that was pulling his cows down from the trees and Mrs. Reed's eggs that had gone off."

Looking at his uncle, Crispin could tell by the twinkle in his eye that he was in no serious difficulty. Nevertheless, he felt he ought to apologize. He said, "I *am* sorry. I'm afraid we lost our heads. From now on we'll stick to the paths. But Vortex *does* love to jump, doesn't he!"

"Indeed he does, and you don't do half-badly yourself but, instead of the local countryside, you had better take Vortex into the forest. He knows that territory much better anyway. And any time you think you're lost, just give him his head and he will bring you out by the shortest route."

So it was that Crispin reentered the forest. Not where he had entered it the first time, a month or so ago, but at the opposite side. He and Vortex turned out of the stable yard of the Legendary Boar past a bay tree, from which he picked a leaf. They clattered splashing into the shallow water of the ford, sending jets of wet light into the sunshine. The boy dropped the leaf into the water and then they disappeared into the high shades and shadows of the forest. The boy figured that, if there was a track at his side of the forest, as there was, there would certainly be one at his uncle's end. There was such a track and the horse needed no urging to follow it. They loped along through glooms and glades, and sometimes through open meadows. Because the forest had been left unmanaged for the hundreds of years during the ban, dead trees leaned like parasites against living ones, and the undergrowth had sprung up uncontested except by shade. But no matter how far the trees retreated from the trail, or how closely they closed in upon it, there was no longer the sense of watchful stillness and waiting that there had been the first time he entered the forest, and before he lifted the ban.

* * *

Back at the Longshanks luncheon, Sarah had her tongue in her cheek. "You mean you jump cows as well as hen houses?" Everybody laughed at the thought, even McGuiness, who had been waiting impatiently by the sideboard, lost his steely look, but only for a moment.

"I think we should go out on the lawn," said Sarah, "and let Mac finish up in here."

So out they went.

"Now tell me more about that umbrella that you mentioned before lunch. It sounds most interesting."

Crispin read immediately the thought at the back of the girl's mind, and he rehearsed carefully for her the different times he had used the umbrella himself. Then he waited for her question.

Sarah asked, "It would take me where I might want to go. Would it take my wheelchair?"

"I don't know. We could ask Blight, and even if he doesn't know, we could certainly give it a try."

However, Blight was deep in conversation with Colonel Falkrest on the efficient running of large establishments and both Crispin and Sarah felt they should not interrupt. When that conversation came to an end, it was time to go and Crispin and Blight drove off in the Pierce Arrow, waving goodbye to Sarah and her father and promising to return soon.

"And I'll bring Tarquin next time," the boy shouted from the car window.

* * *

In a short time, they were being cranked across the estuary from Shanksmare to County Tryce on the Wider Water Ferry. The ferryman and his boy did the cranking. Standing next to the car, Crispin noticed that the ferryman's boy could spit through his teeth. This was a trick that Crispin had not been able to master. He regarded the ferryman's boy with some envy. Tarquin could do it, but then, he *would*; he could whistle between his teeth, too. The boy wondered whether Blight could do it, but decided not to ask, at least not then. Instead he asked, "Blight, do you think the umbrella could move both Sarah and her wheelchair?"

"Guess what? I have been asking myself that very same question."

"And?"

"I don't really know. I don't see any reason why not, but as far as I know, it has never been tried. You were thinking of trying it."

"Yes. I should like to very much. And it would be great for Sarah."

"Give her a change of scene."

"Yes. We could go anywhere; and take Tarquin to help with the chair."

"Perhaps you should ask your friend Greyfell the wolf, since he is the Guardian of the Forest, or was until the ban was lifted. Where *is* the umbrella, by the way?"

"You were the last one to use it."

"So I was. Let me think. I folded it up and put it down next to me in the needles under your great tree. In the excitement of your saving the tree from its galloping disease, and all that followed, I completely forgot about it. So, either it is still lying there or Greyfell took care of it. Unless somebody else picked it up. But we would have known about that."

They reached the shore, got back into the car, waited for the few other passengers to disembark, and then rolled gently off the ferry and up the steep bank and sped away. They went back the way they had come, along county roads, through Chewing Cud (it was not market day), zipping down country lanes through splashes of sunshine and shadow, looping past Priorfields and finally pulling through the big arched gateway into the cobbled yard of Crispin's home, Agincroft, his family name.

The boy got out and patted the side of the silvery-green auto as though it were an animal, and said, "Thank you Blight for taking the day off."

"My pleasure. Keep me posted on developments." He put the car in reverse, backed around and drove out, disappearing through the arched gateway.

* * *

Crispin found Greyfell where he had found him first, under the great pine tree. But the tripod, the cauldron, and the fire that had flickered under it were all gone. The old wolf sat beneath the tree, as it were 'on guard,' looking even older and wiser than before. Thinner and greyer, but his eyes snapped with the same yellow fire as when the boy had first looked into them.

"You have been learning to ride," said the wolf when Crispin apologized for not returning sooner.

"How did you know that?"

"In my rambles I have seen you on Vortex, and heard, anyway, the sound of his hoof beats. They are not nearly the same as when your uncle is in the saddle. You are learning the forest from Vortex. That is a good way. It will give you the skeleton, the paths and trails. Very necessary, but not all."

"Would you please show me what I would be missing?" asked the boy.

"I would like that, but you have not come to ask about the forest." As he said this, all expression drained from Greyfell's face so that it became an inscrutable blank.

Crispin regarded the old wolf thoughtfully. "The umbrella," he asked, "besides people, could it take other things, like things they were sitting in?"

"Go on," said Greyfell quietly.

"There is a girl, Sarah, who is confined to a wheelchair . . ."

"A wheel chair?"

"Yes. She has had Infantile Paralysis and cannot walk. The wheelchair helps her to get around, but it is slow and awkward. She cannot really leave Longshanks Hall, so, if the umbrella will take . . ."

"Anything you are carrying, or that is carrying you."

"*Any*thing?"

"I suppose there are reasonable limits. But a wheel chair, if I understand you, would fall within the limits. Certainly . . . I would think. Considering the state of the girl."

"In that case, I would like to borrow that umbrella again, if I might."

"There is no need for you to ask." The wolf looked into Crispin's eyes a deep, searching look. "There is great goodness in you, and a growing wisdom. *You* see, at times, what is hidden from others, but your quick temper interferes. Growth will help that, rather than make it worse."

"Mother says I'm bound to start growing because my feet are big."

Greyfell cocked an eyebrow and smiled. "Mothers know many things, and can speak them correctly, so they should be listened to. Your mother is one of the wiser, and it was of wisdom that I spoke, the wisdom that can grow with experience.

"Now, about the umbrella there are some things that I can tell you. It is not part of the forest; the umbrella is greater than the forest. You know that it can transport you from place to place; it can also transport you in time."

The boy's eyes widened.

"That is, you can go back anywhere into the past to do what must be done, but not into your *own* past, either to see yourself in the third person, or to become what you have already been, which would be pointless."

The boy considered this information with wonder. "And will it take me into the future?" he asked.

"No, no, no, no! Not the future. Never the future. That would be terrible." The wolf looked troubled and uneasy. "The future is the country of hope and bright promise because it is expected but unknown, and so it must remain. Besides, there is no return from the future into the present."

"But if I can go back into the past and return, why can't I go forward and return to the present."

"Because the past is always with us, but the future is not yet. Because the past is *finished*, although incomplete. If you go into the future you will simply become what you will be, and there is no return from that. Come, let me get it for you."

The old wolf sprang to his feet with an agility still youthful and together he and the boy circled the vast tree until they came to the place where the umbrella lay hidden among the gnarled roots. Greyfell drew it forth and sat down again, placing it beside him on the deep bed of pine needles. Crispin stood close up to the trunk, with one hand on the bark, gazing straight up until the trunk disappeared among clouds of green needles. He thought, *The only way to learn a tree is by climbing it..* Then he turned back to the wolf and said, "The only way to learn a tree is by climbing it."

"All very well for you climbers. It's the aspiration to go beyond yourselves, I suppose. The forest floor is challenge enough for wolves. Perhaps that is why the umbrella is useless to me. However, let me advise you against idle curiosity, whims, or trivialities. You might get more than you bargained for or anticipated. The power that operates the umbrella is benevolent, but not to be taken lightly."

"What power is that?"

"It is a power, I believe, that you must learn as you go along. It cannot be spoken all at once, or described. Above all, it cannot be named. That is as much as I can tell you. I do not use the umbrella; there is no need for me to do so. So take it with you, by all means, but use it wisely."

With that he turned the dark green umbrella over to the boy. It was just the shade of the needles on the great tree. But Crispin said, "You sound so solemn and serious I'm not sure I want to use it at all."

Greyfell nodded. "That would be very safe. Like never climbing a tree. You surely have heard the expression, 'Nothing ventured, nothing gained'? Think of it as a venture; not an *ad*venture but a venture, like learning. Some things grow better through use, and when you are ready to learn the rest of the forest, come back and you will see what *I* can do for you."

FOUR

TRIAL RUNS

It worked! The umbrella moved Sarah and her wheelchair from the library to the center of the lawn outside the windows, leaving Crispin to collapse the umbrella and both to rush out and join the elated girl. Not too many minutes earlier, first the older brother and then the younger brother had materialized on the same lawn outside the windows. They had been standing together in Crispin's room while the younger boy explained the workings of the umbrella very carefully to his older brother.

"If you open it all the way so that it clicks at the top, and say where you would like to go, the umbrella will stay behind. So, depending on where you wind up, you won't be able to get back in a hurry."

"Is that what happened to you when you were locked in your room?"

"Yes, because I was angry and in a hurry, so I did what I had learned first. But if you want to take the umbrella with you, put it up almost all the way and then slowly begin to bring it down, saying where you want to go, and it will come with you. So it doesn't pay to get angry."

"Or to be in a big hurry."

"Right. Are you ready to go?"

Tarquin looked doubtfully at the umbrella. Running very delicately around the fringes of his mind was the suspicion that his younger brother might be playing a trick so that he could laugh at

Tarquin's simple gullibility. He said, "Why don't you give me a demonstration."

"You don't believe me."

"I didn't say that."

"You didn't have to. All right, I'll go first."

"No, no. I'll take a trial spin," and he snapped open the umbrella and, holding it over his head, said, "Take me to my bedroom," and disappeared.

The umbrella remained suspended in midair for a moment and the boy took it by the handle before it hit the ground. He shut it and rushed through the bathroom into Tarquin's room. He wasn't there. "Tarquin, where are you?" he cried.

"I'm under here." And he crawled out from underneath the bed. Then it was, for the very first time, that it occurred to Crispin that whatever power was at work in the umbrella might have a sense of humor.

What he said was, "You probably should have said, *please*."

"Never mind. C'mon, let's go to Longshanks, or wherever this place is."

Off they went. This time Tarquin said *please*, so *that* worked all right, and Crispin remembered to bring the umbrella with him.

Now the two brothers rushed out onto the lawn to where Sarah was pounding the arms of her wheelchair.

"This is positively duplex! It's more, it's triplex! How does it work? How can it work? Somebody better pinch me." Her face shone with such a light that she almost looked like a different girl.

"Well, at least you didn't wind up under the bed," Tarquin remarked, but with good humor.

Sarah looked quizzically at Crispin, who innocently widened his eyes and then winked at the girl.

"Extraordinary," she said, holding out her hand for the umbrella, "there is nothing about this umbrella that makes it look different from any other that I have ever seen," and clicking it open.

Crispin took the umbrella gently from the girl and collapsed it again. "This umbrella is even more amazing than we have experienced so far," he said. "You had better let me tell you what Greyfell told me when I went to borrow it." He furled the umbrella tightly and snapped the tab around it. Both Sarah and Tarquin could see that he looked very serious, so they settled themselves to listen.

He told them everything Greyfell had said about the umbrella and using it wisely, but nothing that the wolf had said about the boy himself. Then the three were silent, until Crispin added, "Nothing ventured, nothing gained."

"Where does that leave us?" asked Tarquin, all businesslike.

"I would like to know how the Leopard of Tryce planned to get even with Chase Longshanks. Dads doesn't know, and the ledgers are no good; they're all numbers."

Tarquin looked puzzled, so Sarah and Crispin recounted the story that Colonel Falkrest had told them over lunch more than a week ago.

"Oh yeah, that sounds pretty interesting; let's give that a try." Tarquin was not a follower; he was a leader. He liked to come up with the suggestions and he generally liked his own suggestions better than anyone else's. He was having a difficult day but behaving well in a strange house with a girl in a wheelchair.

"Where do you think we ought to start?" asked Crispin, whose instincts about his older brother were usually pretty sound.

"Tryceholdings Guard. The castle was the center of everything, at least according to you, so maybe we should start there."

Crispin had been given a tour of the castle, now the County Seat, by his parents' friend, Joshua M. P. Runnel, the Tryce County Archivist. The boy enjoyed that immensely, and especially the grizzly tale of the Archduke's death and burial.

* * *

Josh Runnel, the archivist, had started with some information the boy already knew: "Tryceholdings Guard was the seat of County Tryce. It had formerly been the seat of the Archdukes of Tryce, who ruled the vast holdings of the Archduchy from this great castle at the top of the town." But then he continued: "After two centuries of rule and misrule, the end of the family line finally arrived. The body of Archduke Axel, known as the 'Leopard of Tryce,' was brought back to the castle on a litter between two horses. Soon the manner of his death passed from one to another of the townsfolk in horrified whispers. He had been out hunting alone in the forest and was overtaken both by darkness and by wolves. The wolves, or wolf, had savagely torn out his throat, but left the rest of him intact.

"With great reluctance Bishop Trycewinning agreed to do the funeral, but the cathedral was empty of mourners except for a few of the morbidly curious, and two of the Leopard's henchmen. With even greater reluctance the Bishop agreed that the coffin should be lowered into the Tryce family crypt beneath the floor of the cathedral. 'The man should be buried beneath a crossroad where the tread of travelers would pass over his head,' said the bishop, according to report.

"After the burial of the last Archduke, the few remaining inhabitants of the castle fled, leaving Tryceholdings Guard deserted and gaping. The portcullis was up; the drawbridge was down. Nobody went in. It remained that way for some days, the good people of the town not daring, nor wishing to enter a pile with such a reputation, a reputation fast converting to the rumor that the place was haunted by the Leopard himself, with his throat torn out by wolves. People stopped at the foot of the drawbridge and peered up through the raised portcullis. Then they blessed themselves and hurried away.

"A solitary cat, they say, was first across the drawbridge and disappeared in search of castle rats and mice. A day or two later it was seen sunning itself atop one of the towers. Then, by ones and twos, the poorest people of the town crept in by night, staking squatters' claims to various rooms and apartments. It did them no good. They were dispersed by a procession of town and county officials, led by the High Sherriff and the Mayor in full regalia, taking formal possession. Then the bishop came, accompanied by acolytes with candles and incense; he splattered holy water, exorcising and blessing the entire castle from dungeons (they found no skeletons) to towers. Gradually county and town offices multiplied and took over the castle completely."

* * *

Crispin thought he would save this story for some dark night by firelight. Instead, he said to Tarquin, "OK, you blaze the trail, then Sarah, and I'll bring the umbrella."

"No. Count me out," said the girl.

"But aren't you coming with us?"

"Not this time. You don't know what it's going to be like in the castle with a girl in a wheelchair. You might have to move very quickly or run. And I think there ought to be someone at this end who knows where you've gone. In case."

"I guess you're right about the wheelchair, if what my brother tells me is true. I mean, narrow circular stairways. That sort of thing."

Crispin took him up, "But I don't think you're right about the 'in case.' We can trust the umbrella; I'm sure of it. Could you change your mind?"

"Not this time. Next time."

And so it happened that only the two brothers materialized on the battlements of Tryceholdings Guard that chill, windy midnight, and returned, after their discovery of the Leopard's conspiracy, to Sarah and the sunny lawns of Longshanks Hall.

FIVE

THE BROTHERS TRYCE

At nine o'clock the sky was still light. As a young boy not quite eight, Crispin had been sent upstairs to go to bed. He was in his room, wending his way in the direction of bed, but slowly.

"Crispin, are you in bed yet?" His father's voice called from down the tower stairs.

"Almost," he called back, stretching it a bit. Well, he *had* finished brushing his teeth, and he *did* have his shoes and socks off, feeling the hardwood floor lovely and cool under his bare feet. His book lay open on the window seat next to his bed and he could feel its tug, but he was holding the book in reserve. Ever since his quest he had become more careful of time. He took off his clothes and put on his blue-striped pajama pants and hung up his shorts and shirt in the closet. There had been times when he was made to get out of bed and hang up his clothes, so now he mostly did it without thinking about it.

He went into the bathroom and washed, first taking off the fine gold chain with the Ring of Harklinden on it. This was the ring the Abbot, Blaise, had given him on the completion of his quest and the lifting of the ban. He piled it carefully on the lip of the washbowl, took his washcloth and plunged it in the water and scrubbed away at his face, neck, and ears, shutting his eyes tight to keep out the soap. His parents would not send Tarquin up to bed until they were sure he was out of the bathroom. That saved struggle and stress at the washbowl. He also knew that his brother would not mind how long he took going to bed. He toweled himself dry, put the chain and ring back on, brushed his hair a bit, turned out the light and closed the bathroom door. Then he dropped the pajama top over his head and made a grab for his pants. The pajamas had been bought a size or two large in expectation of growth, so he was continually pulling up his drawers and rolling back his sleeves.

Through this process the boy's mind had been circling above the umbrella at the back of his closet. By no means did 'out of sight' mean 'out of mind.' The fascination lay in the fact that he could visit the past and return to his room at the loss of only a second. No one would know he had been gone nor for how long. Provided, that is, he could get back. But with the umbrella there would be no problem. Would there? He wished he had someone to take with him. Tarquin was practical and thoroughly matter-of-fact and therefore no fun. He wondered what Blight was doing. Reading his theology, probably. Wise Blight, who knew what the boy was thinking, sometimes before he knew it himself.

He went to the window seat, climbed onto it, hooked his left arm around the center window post and leaned out. The sky was beginning to lose light. The boy gazed up and saw a fleeting shape swinging across the blue. Just in case, he leaned out further and held up his right fist, at the same time sliding a finger of his left hand through the ring on his chest. Yes, within a minute the bird had dropped onto his fist and become Malgrin the falcon.

"Malgrin, how great to see you again," he exclaimed.

"I was wondering which room was yours and was just about to try one or two when you leaned out."

"You were looking for me? Is anything wrong?"

Malgrin's yellow-rimmed eyes shot out glints as he said, "I can't see what it is. But I can feel it, here," and he stretched out his wings so that the feathers fanned out. "There are currents in the air, threads from beyond that I can only read through my feathers.

I have spoken to Greyfell about it. He doesn't feel it, but he hears it, the echo of hoof beats, he says. Not present hoof beats, but from the past. He sent me to you. 'It is only Crispin who will do something.' His very words."

"But what am I supposed to do?" Forgetting the bird on his fist, he sat down suddenly and crossed his legs so that Malgrin had to re-alight on the window sill.

"That is what I asked Greyfell. What is that noise?"

"You asked Greyfell, 'What is that noise?'"

"No, that noise in your room; what is that?"

"Oh, that's only my brother in the bathroom. He's getting ready for bed, drawing water in the bowl. What did Greyfell say?"

"Use the umbrella; tell Crispin to use the umbrella."

"I knew it; I knew it; I could feel it in my blood. You in your wings and Greyfell in his ears and me in my blood."

The bathroom door opened but before Tarquin could set foot in the bedroom the falcon had dropped off the sill, darted across the courtyard and was gone.

"Who are you talking to in here?" asked his brother.

"Nobody. Myself."

"You must have money in the bank," an expression the older boy had heard his parents use for people who talked to themselves. "It's after nine-thirty, lights-out time. They'll be up any minute to check." He had a way of turning everything into a "we-they" situation.

"I was just thinking about getting into bed when you came in."

"Oh sure. Well, don't fall out the window."

Tarquin went back through the bathroom to his own room, closing Crispin's door behind him. *Forewarned is forearmed*, the boy said to himself, so he got into bed with his back to the door and his head turned so that he could see out the window. He lay still until he heard his bedroom door open softly and then close again. Had it been his mother or his father? It made no difference. He threw off the bed clothes and got up. He dressed swiftly, pulled his old blue sweater on, remembering the chill wind on the castle ramparts, and reached into the back of his closet for the umbrella.

Then he stopped. Where should he go? Should he consult with Greyfell first? No. Clearly Greyfell expected him to know. What was he sure of? He knew that the Leopard of Tryce was going to the abbey to inflict the ban on his brother, Blaise. That was all he had to go on, so that was where he would go. He opened the umbrella carefully, but not all the way. Then, just as he started to close it again, he said, "Please, to the meeting of Abbot Blaise and the Archduke."

* * *

He thought he would be somewhere in the abbey building but he was in the forest. He collapsed the umbrella and looked about. The place looked familiar but somehow very different. Immediately in front of him was a curving wall made up of massive stone blocks and a broad stone stairway leading upwards. Of course. It was the large circular terrace at the center of which stood his great tree. Crispin could not see over the high wall so he set down the umbrella and slithered his way up the steps, crouching low. With infinite care he raised his head above the last step, and gasped.

His great tree was not there! In its place stood a young pine barely one hundred feet tall. Then he realized that this *was* his tree, but centuries ago. Small wonder that the sun blazed unimpeded on his back. No thick bed of brown pine needles surrounded the tree but lush green grass rose up the gentle incline to the tree at the center. Beneath the tree stood the Abbot Blaise with a broom over his shoulder very much as Crispin would have carried a baseball bat. The boy recognized the abbot at once even though he was wearing a dusky work-habit and cowl. He was thinking of hailing him when he heard a familiar jingling and clinking noise approaching rapidly from the other side of the terrace.

He lowered his head and worked his way back down the stairs. With the advent of the Leopard he had felt unprotected and vulnerable where he was. Instead he found a couple of toeholds among the massive stones of the wall so that he could just get his eyes above the wall but still be partially screened by the grasses.

Across the terrace, the Leopard spurred his horse up the steps. The horse was a lanky, powerful, black brute that the boy felt sure must be Backlash. Dorn and the other henchman remained below the circle. The Leopard, sounding like a man who knows he holds the winning cards, wasted no time.

"I have come one last time, brother Blaise, to inquire whether you will permit passage of myself and a few friends through your domain."

"Your persistence is admirable," said the Abbot, "especially when not accompanied by threats. One can only hope that you will find my own perseverance equally admirable. The answer is 'No.'"

"Even if I give you my solemn word?"

"What on earth have you ever done," exclaimed Blaise, "that would encourage me to trust your word? Solemn or otherwise."

"Alas, dear brother, I have done my best for you, even to the point of trying to save you from catastrophe."

"What catastrophe?" he asked, taking the broom from his shoulder, an action that made Backlash dance nervously to one side.

The younger brother patted the horse's neck, gentling it, and then, unbuttoning his doublet, drew out the packet that Crispin had seen before in Tryceholdings Guard. "It has become my so very painful duty," said the Leopard, "to apprise you of the regrettable fact that no longer will you be the 'Grey Wolf of Harklinden.' One week from this very day the Abbey of Our Lady of Harklinden, its abbot, its monks, and all of its buildings and outbuildings lying within the forest, are to be placed under a ban; all the aforesaid buildings and lands to be administered by the currently reigning Archduke of Tryce. Behold the papal document!" He opened up the large vellum sheet with dangling seals at the bottom and held it up.

"May I see it?"

"Why ever not?"

The document changed hands. The Abbot Blaise read it more than once, Crispin felt, and then refolded it carefully and handed it back. Then he said, "Axel, I know not what lies you have told, nor what bribes you have paid, nor pressures brought to bear on the Holy See, or on Bishop Trycewinning . . . ," he stopped. Then, with infinite irony, sadness, and contempt, he repeated, "Trycewinning!" The boy in hiding felt a lump form in his own throat and he had to grit his teeth to keep from crying out.

In a voice clouded with emotion, Blaise said, "You think you have won . . . "

"I *know* I have won."

" . . . and that you will be able to use this forest as you did Trycemeadows, for your own wasteful, wicked purposes. But let me warn *you*." Here he took the broom and, making a seeping movement through the air, continued, "with something as simple as this broom, I will work to foil your every device and erase your every design."

"Oh no you won't," cried the Leopard, drawing his sword and raising it above his brother's head. But Blaise stood his ground, unflinching.

"Go ahead! That is so like you, Axel, to strike down an unarmed man. Your courage was always notable, if only for its absence."

Stung, the Leopard spurred his horse to the tree and, with a heavy stroke, lopped off a sapling branch. "And I," he bellowed, "with a broom made from this branch and wound about with spells, will have my own way. And remember, you and your monks must be out of here in a week, or suffer the mortal consequences. You see, leopards can outrun wolves any day of the week."

"But wolves are wiser. And they live longer."

Abbot Blaise shouldered his broom and strode across the terrace in the direction of the abbey. Crispin saw him go down the steps opposite and pass between the two henchmen as though they did not exist. The Archduke watched him go, then he motioned to his men, wheeled his horse around and headed towards the steps near which Crispin was watching. The boy dropped noiselessly off the wall and crawled under the tall ferns that grew up close to the huge retaining stones.

The umbrella! Where was the umbrella? He had left it at the bottom of the steps when he had first worked his way up. It must be in plain sight. But there was no time to retrieve it. He could hear one of the men jogging his horse around the perimeter of the circle on his side. He pushed even further among the ferns, afraid that the horse might step on him, and pulled the fronds over his crouching body. He could hear Backlash picking his way down the steps, and he held his breath. He could feel himself starting to shake.

The one horse and rider passed so close to the concealed boy that the smell of the horse enveloped him and he thought he most certainly would be discovered. But horse and rider moved on. From his hiding place he could not see the meeting of the three horsemen. So far they had not spotted the umbrella. Gently he let his breath out, and breathed again, until he heard the Leopard of Tryce say, "You know your instructions. Tell my friends to meet me one week from tonight. At Agincroft."

SIX

APPEARING AND DISAPPEARING

Crispin arrived back in his bedroom badly shaken. How horrible to think of that evil man here in his own home, and his three miserable companions with who knows how many followers. The boy climbed onto his bed and looked around his darkening room. Minutes ago it had seemed like the safest of safe havens, and now . . . . He got up and turned on all the lights. That helped disperse the gathering shadows and restore what was safe because most familiar. He snapped the umbrella and put it against the back wall of his closet. Then he turned out all the lights except the one next to his bed, and went into the bathroom. Very cautiously he opened the door into his brother's room.

"Tarquin, are you awake?" he whispered hoarsely.

"Yes. Come in. What were you doing with all your lights on? They were shining down into the courtyard, a dead giveaway that you're still up."

His brother was not in bed but lying on his window seat, propped up by his pillows. Crispin walked around the end of the bed and hoisted himself up on it.

"You have all your clothes back on!" Tarquin sat upright. "Have you *been* out, or are you going?"

"I just got back. That's why I came in. I don't know what to do; I need your advice." He had found the shortest way around an older brother – ask for his advice. So he recounted where he had just been and what had happened, and Tarquin rose to the bait and took it.

"D'you mean that lousy guy is coming to our house? And bringing his lackey friends? Over my dead body! When is this supposed to take place?"

"It's the night of the day when the ban takes effect."

"Oh, right. That means the entire forest will be open for the old Leopard and his buddies to pass through."

Needless to say, Crispin was delighted that his brother had plunged right in and seemed no longer concerned that he was dealing with an episode that had already taken place. The younger boy did not want to remind him of that fact for fear he would give up entirely. So he asked a question instead.

"Do you think we should learn their plans?"

"If we did that I suppose we could warn what's his name, Chase Longshanks, in case he doesn't know or even suspect. And also who's ever keeping the ford."

Tarquin had gotten up from the window seat and was pacing around his room so that his bare feet went slap, slap on the wood floor. On one of these turns he glanced out his window and said, "You'd better turn your light off or Dad will be in to see what's going on. And if he finds you with your clothes on there'll be hell to pay."

Tarquin was just at that age when he had started to absorb colorful expressions from his friends at school, expressions he was careful not to use around his parents. Crispin hopped down from the bed and went into his room. He got back into his pajamas, hung up his clothes for the second time that night and went around to turn off the light. Just as he was reaching for it his door opened. It was his mother.

"Why is your light on? Have you been reading again? You should have been asleep long ago. What's going on?"

Crispin was tempted to respond (as Greyfell had once responded to him), "That's three questions. Which one first?" But he rejected that idea instantly and said, instead, "I'm sorry. I was just talking to Tarquin." He turned off the light and continued, "I'm almost asleep already," and climbed into bed.

"Well, don't forget to say your payers, but don't get out of bed. Just get to sleep as quickly as you can manage it." His mother quietly closed the door into the bathroom and then went out and closed Crispin's door. The boy listened intently as he ran through his prayers by rote. No, Tarquin's door was not opened. That was a relief. Then he remembered those painted eyes that had looked into his from the chapel wall at Tryceholdings Guard, the eyes of Christ on the cross, so he started his prayers again. But he had not even gotten through the Our Father before he was completely adrift in sleep.

* * *

The next morning both boys were somewhat late for breakfast. Their father, who was just leaving for town when they came in, exchanged a raised eyebrow with their mother. Unfortunately the boys were even later finishing, which was worse. They sat across from one another, eating silently. Then, without looking up from his plate, Tarquin said quietly, "I've been thinking about our problem. We had better make sure we learn their plans. That means we can't nix their meeting here. But just wait till they make their next move; we'll be way ahead of them."

"Do you think we should include Sarah? She said she'd go next time."

Tarquin was silent, chewing thoughtfully. "There's already been a 'next time.'"

"You can't count last night." Crispin stirred his cocoa and then licked his spoon. "Can you?" He watched his brother carefully over the rim of his cup as he drank. Tarquin pushed his empty plate away and sat back in his chair.

"Why not?"

"Because we didn't plan it or anything. It was Malgrin who encouraged me to do something. So I did."

The older boy was silent for a time, then he said, "I suppose she can go. She seems like a sensible enough girl. And she knows everything about Longshanks Hall, which may help. But the wheelchair's a problem."

"Should I keep Blight informed?" Crispin continued to defer to his brother's judgment, thinking (correctly) that this would make him feel like the leader in charge.

"Definitely. He may turn out to be one of our key players."

"Then I'll see if I can hunt him up this morning. He asked me to keep him posted. He may be able to tell us something we don't already know."

"Yeah, more likely *we* can tell *him*. But, you gather the information and we'll pool our resources."

"Crispin opened his mouth to reply but shut it again because his mother came through from the kitchen.

"If you two night owls have finished, clear off the table, please, and bring the dishes out. I want to do them before Henriette gets here." Then she looked at Tarquin directly. "This is your day to mow the terrace lawn, remember. Your brother can hold up the evergreen branches with a rake so you can cut underneath."

"Oh, Mom, can't it go for another day?"

"Do it today, it needs it. Now brush your teeth and get busy before I think of something more for you to do."

* * *

Crispin discovered Blight hard at work on his theology in the library of the abbey.

Nevertheless, Blight had discovered a map.

"Well, Crispin, it stood to reason that there was one. My brothers in Christ, those monks of old, kept track of everything: building and planting, cutting and pruning, buying and selling, you name it. There are separate accounts for each of the cells out in the forest, each according to a Saint's name. But the accounts didn't tell me which one was which, so I knew there must be a map. And here it is."

He reached behind him and pulled forth a long roll of parchment which he unrolled on a large library table. It was not at all the kind of map the boy was used to. More important things were larger and less important smaller; the distances were anything but according to scale. At the very center was a large, spidery drawing of what must be the Abbey. Blight pointed out the boy's own house, small, and Priorfields, considerably larger.

"But this map doesn't seem useful at all."

"Once you get used to the way it's drawn, interesting things begin to turn up. For example, here is the ford, up here at the top because the whole map is drawn from an imaginary viewpoint facing the abbey. What looks like a straight river here is actually the road from Shipman's Brink, very important for building the Abbey, whereas this little thread squirreling its way down here is the track from the Ford. But notice this dotted line that connects these cells, each cell carefully labeled with its saint's name; see how it makes a much shorter route between Abbey and Ford? *If* one could discover it. I wonder if your Uncle Fritz knows about this short cut. I haven't had a chance to ask him yet."

"I'll bet Greyfell knows; he told me he could show me a thing or two that Vortex wouldn't know. Uncle Fritz would let me borrow Vortex and with you on Nightmare – "

"The question right now is, are we going to need a short cut?"

"I don't know. We won't know their plans until we listen in on their meeting; we haven't done that yet. We don't even know whether it will be possible. We're going to give it a try this afternoon."

"Well, keep a cool head and don't take any chances. Your uncle and I have a meeting with the bishop this afternoon. He wants to assess our progress. You wouldn't think I'd be nervous but I am. So if you can fit in a prayer for the two of us that would be helpful."

Crispin looked at Blight. For the first time he noticed a preoccupied look that he had never seen before, and furrows between his eyebrows. "You mean this is like a test?" he asked.

"Not exactly. I think it's being billed as 'a learned conversation.'"

"Blight, you will do splendidly. I know it. You've practically eaten these books alive."

"Ah, but the question is, 'How much have I digested?'"

"Don't worry. If there's any trouble you send the bishop to me."

Blight laughed, he actually did. "You're beginning to sound like Tarquin," he said.

* * *

Crispin's next stop was Greyfell.

"The short cut from the abbey to the ford? Yes, I know it well. It connects the three cells on the upland plateau. It hasn't been used for ages, except, occasionally, by my family, and by deer. It would be invisible to anyone, even if they were looking for it, although it is perfectly plain to us."

"Even to Blight?" asked the boy.

"Even to Blight."

"Could you show it to me, in case we have to use it?"

"I couldn't. Not any more. But I can do better than that. I can have one of my grandsons guide you. Torfell would be best, I think. He has wanted to meet you anyway."

"But, I didn't know you had grandchildren," the boy exclaimed. "I didn't even know you had children. Why haven't you introduced me"?

"There has never really been time or opportunity. But you let me know when you want to ride the short cut and I will send Torfell to meet you at the ford."

"I have to get permission to stay with my uncle first, at both ends, home and at the ford. I don't know what to tell you."

"Never mind. My family network is more than reliable. When you arrive at the ford, we will know about it. Just get on Vortex when you're ready, and cross the ford. One other thing; it might be a good idea to prepare Vortex to meet Torfell," and the old wolf smiled, but a very un-wolflike smile.

* * *

"Oh, great!" exclaimed Sarah. "I was hoping you two would turn up. The prospect of getting out of Longshanks for awhile looks better and better."

"Here's the deal," said Tarquin. He proceeded to relate everything that had happened since their last meeting; he got it all right. There were times when Crispin actually felt proud to be Tarquin's brother and this was one of them.

"And they're meeting in *your* house! We thought it was only the Hall that had to put up with the Leopard. I *am* sorry."

"Never mind. It's the meeting we want to get to. Now, where do you think is the best place to set you down in your chair? Crispin?"

"Not outside. There may be hundreds of the Archduke's men-at-arms milling about." Tarquin looked askance at his brother and his tendency to exaggerate.

"OK. Where inside?"

"Upstairs. We're most familiar with our rooms, so why not there?"

"Sarah?"

"You know your house better than I do."

"Yes. OK. Upstairs it is. Crispin, why don't you go first this time? And I'll bring the umbrella with me."

The younger boy hesitated. He was responsible for the umbrella and he did not want to shirk that. Then Sarah spoke up, "I'll go first since I didn't go at all last time. No, really, I don't mind; in fact, I'd rather, and then Tarquin, you next because Crispin is responsible for the umbrella, I think." Shrewd girl.

Crispin opened the umbrella until it clicked and then handed it to the girl. "What directions should I give?" she asked.

"To the Leopard's meeting at Agincroft, second floor. Please."

Those are the directions she gave, and she disappeared. Her wheelchair, however, did not.

"That's not what Greyfell told me would happen," exclaimed Crispin, appalled at what might have happened to Sarah.

Tarquin had caught the umbrella and held it over his head. He looked at his brother and said, "Try to bring the wheelchair with you, and don't for-. . . never mind." He gave the same directions and disappeared. Crispin took the umbrella in midair, un-clicked the catch, and sat down in the wheelchair. Then, while starting to close the umbrella, repeated the same directions.

In a moment, with the rushing sound of winds and waters still in his ears, he stood in a large, dark room beside his brother. Once again the wheelchair had been left behind, and Sarah was nowhere to be seen.

SEVEN

TRYING TO STAY ONE JUMP AHEAD

"Sarah? Where's Sarah?" Crispin's hoarse whisper echoed in the big room.

"I don't know. She wasn't here when I got here."

"What can have gone wrong? You don't suppose. . . ."

"I've looked up and down the entire room. We're in the right place all right. It's our rooms before they were divided and the bathroom put in; she's not hiding – there's no place."

"But. . . ."

"Don't jump to conclusions. We'll figure this out."

"Right. But wherever she is, she's all by herself and wondering where we are."

"I know, I know. What have we got to go on?"

"She said exactly the same thing we said."

"And wound up in some other place."

"Or some other time."

"Or both."

"Wait. I think maybe I can use this to find her." Crispin opened the umbrella and, starting to close it – but before he could say anything his brother said, "You better come back with that thing. I don't want to get stuck here for the rest of my life."

"Don't worry, I'll be back. You won't get any older anyway."

"Oh right! That's some consolation!"

Crispin started again, without interruption, and this time he said, "Please take me to wherever Sarah is."

Nothing happened.

Dear God," said Tarquin, "I hope that thing isn't broken."

"It can't be!" Crispin tried again, saying the same thing.

Nothing happened.

Then the door opened and Sarah walked in. "Nice place you have here," she said.

The other two were flabbergasted. They stood there speechless and not believing their eyes. The girl closed the door behind her and said, "You'd better let me tell you what happened and what I've learned."

Crispin felt the need to sit down and backed up against the sleeping platform for pilgrims to the Abbey. He pulled himself onto that, put his elbows on his knees and his head in his hands. After a while he started to breathe normally again. His more stoical brother let out a long, relieved sigh and muttered, "Well I'll be dipped."

"I suppose I have given you rather a bad scare, haven't I? But I couldn't help it. When I arrived, there was a man walking toward me, just a few feet away. Somehow I had landed on my feet and ran out through the open door. I could hear him coming on behind me but he didn't say anything. Then I got to the top of the tower stairs and just ran down that. I was all right! I could do it! I think it must have something to do with the time factor but I can't figure out what.

"Anyway, I could hear the man coming down the stairs behind me and I didn't know where to hide. There was a woman standing at the bottom of the stairs as I came around and she didn't pay any attention to me. Then it struck me – they couldn't see me! I must be invisible!"

"You must be kidding," said Tarquin. "We weren't born yesterday. Or at least *I* wasn't."

"But no, listen. The man came down the stairs; I was flattened against the wall but in plain sight and they both walked right past me. They should have seen me, easily."

"Well, it doesn't seem possible to me. Meanwhile . . ." Tarquin was interrupted by his brother.

"Could they hear you?"

"I don't know. I have my slippers on and they made hardly any noise running down the stairs. What would have happened if I had still been in my chair?"

The older boy began to pace back and forth, shaking his head. The younger was afraid his brother was sorry they had brought Sarah at all, and would say so, but Crispin had had a light. "If we are invisible, that would explain why we weren't discovered at Tryceholdings Guard, not even by the leopards."

That stopped his brother in his tracks. He raised his head and looked at Crispin and smiled. "That's very good," he said. "We should have been seen more than once, at least by the Bishop when he was behind us waiting to be called. Meanwhile, the Leopard may be laying his plans and we're not hearing them."

But the Leopard had not yet arrived. Before they could decide on their next move, they heard a jingling clink from outside, a noise that made the hair rise on the back of Crispin's neck. He went quickly to the window and looked out. Moonlight glistened on the dew-damp cobbles of the yard where a party of horsemen had come in through the big arched gateway. There were at least a dozen of them, as far as he could see. The people downstairs had heard them too, for the front door opened and a rectangle of light spread out under the horse's legs and up their sides.

"Here they are," Crispin exclaimed. "Come on. If we're not invisible we may not find out anything." He took the umbrella and headed for the door, but the other two got there first.

"Let me go ahead and I'll show you what I mean, but try not to make any noise until we're sure about this." Sarah led the way softy but swiftly down the tower stairs. The two boys followed more slowly, from a certain lack of conviction in their own invisibility.

Downstairs was unrecognizable as their home, at first. They stood in a huge kitchen. At this end – a cavernous fireplace with some fowl turning on a spit over the fire and a small boy set to keep them turning. Crispin almost felt as though he had come face-to-face with himself when he saw that boy, but he had no time to reflect. Sarah had walked right out into the middle of the room, carefully avoiding collision with the kitchen workers. The two brothers stepped out warily, then more confidently and joined the girl, looking about with keen interest. Some details they recognized, like the great slabs of the slate floor and the fireplace which did not yet contain Henriette's big stove. Meanwhile the company from outside was already flooding into the hall beyond two stone arches, welcomed by the man Sarah had almost tangled with upstairs.

The first man to enter had pulled his hood well forward so that his face was shadowed; his cloak he had wrapped closely about him so that nothing underneath showed except a very fine riding glove and a length of sleeve in deepest purple. "We are riding on to the Abbey tonight," he was saying, "but just stopped to refresh ourselves with whatever is available."

"You have not heard, then, that the Abbey and the entire forest has been placed under ban?"

"Yes, yes, of course. We heard that as we came along. All of Tryceholdings talks of nothing else. We are going on to assist the poor monks with their departure."

"Then you have *not* heard that all of the Monks have disappeared."

"Disappeared! What do you mean 'disappeared'?"

"That is the word that son Edwin, here, brought earlier this afternoon." The host, Sir Benjamin, stretched out a hand, bringing a younger man into the conversation.

"Yes, that's right," Edwin confirmed. "I had taken over a party of three early in the morning, before word of the ban reached us. But when we arrived at the Abbey we found it deserted. There was nobody there at all."

"You just did not see them, you mean."

No, no, sir, not that at all. We looked very carefully through the entire building, hoping to find someone. There was no one. There were plates on the tables in the refectory, food in the larder, even a fire still burning on the kitchen hearth. But no monks."

"And you saw nothing of the Abbot?"

"The door to his room stood wide open. I looked inside and everything was as I had seen it before, often, to the very ink pots on the table."

"Yes. No doubt you left everything untouched," sneered the hooded figure.

"Indeed I did. I could not even take away his blessing, as I have done before."

"Hiding in the forest, no doubt they are. Out in the cells. Thinking to escape the terms of the ban. Come." He turned to his companions. "We can talk as we ride, but this 'disappearance,' so-called, should be investigated. If the larder is as full as this fellow claims, we can find something to eat when we get there. And perhaps sample the Abbot's cellar." He laughed a grating laugh. "Well, Sir Benjamin is it? We will not require your hospitality after all." And the travelers turned back to the door but made way so that the Archduke could precede them. Crispin had recognized him even before he opened his mouth.

" 'Sir Benjamin is it?' Humpf. Thinks I can't recognize a leopard when I see one. I wonder what he's really up to."

"No good, that one, you can bet your prize pig on that," said his wife, Lady Anne.

Then Edwin said, "I'm sorry I didn't bring the horses back with me."

"How many?" asked his father.

"Just two: one big dappled-grey for hauling logs, and a mare for jogging distances, I would think. Pretty horse."

"Now, Benjamin, best not get mixed up with those horses. Leave them to the Leopard of Tryce to deal with."

"Wife, you are right, as you frequently are."

And Edwin said gleefully, "But wait until he finds there's no bridge, either."

* * *

Crispin, Tarquin, and Sarah had retreated carefully upstairs. They sat in silence in the moon-filled room, listening to the clatter of iron on cobbles as the troop outside left hastily down the track to the bridge, a track plowed under and grown over long before Crispin's day. The room darkened as heavy clouds blew under the moon; then the diminishing clatter of horses got mixed with the splatter of rain on the windows.

"Are we going to leave those two horses to the tender mercies of the Leopard?" asked Sarah.

"What were you thinking of doing with them?" Tarquin asked. "Bringing them back with us?" He looked at the girl with some superiority, as though she had been caught sucking her thumb or biting her nails.

"Crispin?"

"I don't think we should press our luck with the umbrella. Look at what happened with the wheelchair. But we could take them to the ford and leave them with the Guardian."

"Oh sure, with the Leopard and his men breathing down your necks. And suppose he discovers them in the Guardian's barn? He might burn that place down, too."

But Sarah did not think so. "He only plans to pass through the ford, not through the barn. And if the bridge is gone, that would give us plenty of time, wouldn't it?" She turned to the younger boy.

He tried to remember the geography of the forest as he had heard it piecemeal, and seen it on the map that Blight had shown him.

"They would have to go all the way back to Tryceholdings Guard and use the Archduke's Ferry, I think. Or else swim for it."

"That seems unlikely at night. And in this weather." The wind, having hustled-in the clouds, was drawing the rain in swift curtains across the courtyard.

"Well, you can count me out. There are only two horses, anyway, so you won't need me. Just don't get pneumonia." With that, Tarquin reached for the umbrella, opened it until it clicked, and said, "Back to Longshanks, please, and the correct time." He was gone. Crispin collapsed the umbrella.

* * *

The stable of the Abbey was large enough to accommodate the horses of several travelers. It was also warm and dry and dark. Rain thrummed on the slates above; nevertheless it was as watertight as the Ark. Both horses stood at the front of their stalls, heads out and turned in their direction. "Do you suppose they can see us although people can't?" Crispin asked in a low voice.

"Maybe they can just hear us and smell us."

"I wish I had some lump sugar."

"Wait a bit. We're in luck. Here's a whole dish of apples." A wooden bowl of apples had been set down into the mouth of a water barrel. Sarah handed the boy an apple and they advanced down the stable clucking and talking softly to the two horses. Evidently some classical monk had named the two, for the big horse was called Aeneas and the mare, Dido. Their names had been worked in wood and pegged up over their respective stalls. As he had done with Vortex, Crispin kept the apple in one hand behind him and then shifted it to the other so that Aeneas smelt apple on both hands and kept nuzzling him in the chest, in search of the hidden fruit. Sarah was going through the same sort of performance with Dido. But then, while both horses were munching down their apples, all four raised their heads and pricked up their ears. Once again they heard the drumming of horses and the jingle of harness, then the racket of hooves on the stones of the yard and the guttural exclamations of men.

"Oh, Lord! It's the Leopard!"

And the next moment the doors of the stable were thrown open and men and horses trooped in, filling the place with torchlight and noise, damp men and streaming horses.

Instinctively, both Crispin and Sarah dived under the hay, forgetting they were invisible. The Leopard apparently had ways to make bridges reappear other than the leaves of the green bay tree. The boy wondered whether he had used the evil broom that he had threatened Abbot Blaise with. Perhaps he had smacked it down on the river waters and uttered some incantation of his own. What sorts of deeds could those evil powers perform? And where were they watching now? Thank heaven he could travel so much faster with the umbrella. The umbrella? He had left it leaning up against the water barrel. A great hollow opened in the boys' stomach and beads of perspiration broke out across his scalp.

Horny hands had discovered the apples. Some lucky horses got some and the men ate the rest. They dropped the cores where they finished them; horses that could reach them gobbled them down. They rubbed down the horses with straw, and dashed across the courtyard through the rain into the Abbey, taking their torches with them. The last man to leave used his to light a lantern and hang it up over the water barrel. He tipped out the empty bowl onto the floor and discovered the furled umbrella. "Funny looking thing, this," he said to himself. "Must be some monkish foolery." He tucked it under his arm, slurped up some water from his cupped hand, and left, giving the stable door a push with his backside so that it swung shut behind him.

Sarah was already on her feet as Crispin cautiously put aside his covering of straw and stood up beside Aeneas.

"You forgot that they can't see us," she said in a hushed voice. "I forgot for a minute, myself. But he *could* see the umbrella. That's strange."

"We've got to get it back or we're stuck here. Come on!"

"I'm right behind you!" They slid out of the stable door, dashed through the rain and puddles into the great open door of the Abbey.

Crispin had been all over the Abbey with Blight and knew it well. "Here, this door lets us up into the pulpit in the refectory. We can scout from up there. Close the door behind you."

A twist of steps led up into the pulpit, used for reading aloud while the monks ate in the refectory below. The room was not especially large, longer rather than wider, with a simple U-shaped arrangement of tables. When in use, the monks sat only on the outside of the tables; those doing the waiters' tasks served from inside the U. Peering over the edge of the pulpit, the boy was looking down almost directly on the Leopard who, with evident satisfaction, had occupied the Abbot's chair. The same three men Crispin had seen at Tryceholdings Guard were with him now, one on one side and two on the other, their heads leaning together, deep in conversation. Candles burned in front of them among empty cups and the remains of some biscuits. The umbrella lay disregarded on the table in front of the Archduke.

At the lower end of the room, in dim candlelight, the men had seated themselves somewhat sedately on benches, conscious that they were under the eyes of their leaders. They had begun to guzzle pitchers of wine as though they had never had any before.

But they were very aware of the watchful gaze of the Leopard of Tryce and kept control of themselves.

Suddenly the four men at the head of the room pushed back their chairs and stood up, so the entire group sprang to its feet and turned in their direction. The four had picked up their cups and candles and turned to go out the door. But the Archduke paused and turned to the others. He raised his voice in cheerful irony, "Remember, you men, you are within holy walls. If you must sing – hymns only." The four went out, leaving the umbrella lying where it was on the table.

"Quick! Before somebody grabs it," and the boy went swiftly down the stairs, put his ear against the door and listened. No voices, no footsteps. He raised the latch, pushed gently, paused again and listened. No, no sounds. He stepped into the corridor and looked both ways. Nobody. But there was a little light disappearing up the stairs towards the Abbot's room. He stepped along to the door into the refectory, went boldly in, walked to the head table and picked up the umbrella. By this time the men had reseated themselves less formally at the tables and become reoccupied with their refreshment. The volume of noise increased. None of them noticed the umbrella disappearing.

Back in the stable, relieved but feeling the damp, Crispin resolved never to lay the umbrella down again unless he absolutely had to. "That gives us even less time than we had before," he said. "How are we going to get Dido and Aeneas out of here?"

"Good question. It depends on whether there's anyone watching or listening. We should be able to move out of here while they're eating and drinking. That's the best time. We'll have to walk the horses until we get off the paving and maybe even then some. Have you ever ridden bareback?"

"No."

"Well, you're about to learn. Just hang on for dear life with your knees. It would probably be easier if you rode Dido."

"No, it's OK. I've made friends with Aeneas. He'll let me ride him....although he may not know it yet." He fished the chain and the Ring of Harklinden from under his shirt and slid a finger into the ring. In this way he would be sure that Aeneas understood what he was saying and that he, too, would understand the horse.

"Poor beasts aren't going to like this rain much but it seems to be letting up a bit. Let's get on with it before the return of the barbarians."

As they led the two horses slowly and gently across the court, there was a burst of laughter from the refectory and an attempt at the chorus of a song. This covered the click and ring of horseshoe on cobblestones. However, they were soon clear of the stone and onto the rain-softened dirt of the road. Even the arrival of the troop had not stirred it into mud but they could both feel the damp soaking through the canvas of Crispin's shoes and through Sarah's slippers. Somewhere they had to find a place to mount. Sarah felt she might be able to give Crispin a leg up onto Aeneas but she was not at all sure she would be able to scramble onto Dido. The other way round was even less likely.

The track headed off in one direction, then split into two, the eastern track running over to Priorfields and the western doubling back beneath the great terrace on which the Abbey was situated. By great good fortune successive winter frosts had heaved a great stone to the surface at that division. Much of it was still buried in the earth but the top made a high platform from which the boy could vault onto the broad back of Aeneas. Gripping the umbrella in his left hand, he swung over and settled himself on a back as big as a landing field, and patted and smoothed the dappled neck, telling him he was the greatest horse in the world. Then he took the head of Dido and whispered sweet nothings into her ears while Sarah scaled the rock and swung neatly onto her back. The next moment they were away.

They jogged along the track. The rain stopped altogether and some moonlight leaked down through the clouds. "Somebody's going to miss these two horses . . . sooner or later." Crispin was remembering the last time he had traveled this track at midnight. At that time he was walking in the opposite direction with Greyfell. They had almost reached the sheltering trees when they heard a high, shrill whistle, and later they had been pursued by the specter of the Leopard. He kept listening for that signal again, expecting at any moment to hear it piercing the air above them.

"Judging by the rowdy noises they were making, I suspect it will be later rather than sooner," said Sarah. "They won't find out anything until they are ready to mount up. And that may not even be tonight. They may wait another night to give themselves more time. Time to dry out."

"If they still think the monks are hiding-out in the cells," Crispin was thinking aloud, "they will have to fan out and inspect those during daylight."

Nevertheless, they urged their mounts forward. Dido pulled easily ahead, but even Aeneas broke into a long loping canter that put Crispin in danger of falling asleep from the regular motion of the great horse.

EIGHT

BROTHERS BY HALF

In the white dawn, long before sunrise, the ford looked closed up tight and at rest.

Again Crispin was surprised because the place looked so much smaller than he was used to. Yet he recognized the initial low but roomy inn before the many additions he was familiar with had been added. The builders had used the same pale grey stone as at Agincroft, but The Legendary Boar (identified by its sign) fit closer to the ground. It was the barn and stable that dominated the water-meadows. As yet no smoke was ascending from chimneys, no martins or swallows flashed and dipped, no raptors wheeled high above, no hens scratched, but already a rooster was giving a preparatory greeting to encourage the sun.

The two riders had slowed the horses to a walk as they approached.

"Good. There's nobody up yet," said Sarah, and they eased down into the swift water, letting both Dido and Aeneas pause to drink.

"Listen!" Crispin held his arm and hand out towards the girl. From deep in the forest behind them came the sound of galloping horses. "How many?"

"Just three, I think."

"They must be following our trail. Let's move!" Aeneas and Dido had already raised their dripping muzzles and begun to push the rest of the way through the swirling shallows.

"We can't put these two in the barn, too compromising," said Sarah.

"We can't keep going, either. They're bound to catch up with us and then Dido and Aeneas are theirs."

"Let's turn them loose in the meadow and hope. That's all we can do."

So they dropped onto the ground, led the two horses through the meadow gate, and gave each a slap on the rump, which did no good whatsoever. Then they turned to watch the arrival of their pursuers.

"That's Backlash in the lead," said the boy as the three emerged from the trees, still going at a good clip. "The other two are the Leopard's henchmen."

"And the Archduke still in his disguise," added Sarah dryly.

The three riders had to slow for the water lest it trip up their mounts. They did not pause to let the horses drink, but came up the stone ramp with the Leopard leaning out of his saddle, following the damp traces of Dido and Aeneas.

"Of course. There!" He pointed towards the meadow with his riding crop. "Come on, one of you two. Rouse out this Guardian of the Ford."

Not Dorn but the other one, Ulf, swung down from his horse and pounded on the low inn door. Above him The Legendary Boar blazed down from its sign with fiery, piggy eyes. The door opened almost immediately. The man who stepped out looked so much like Archduke Axel that Ulf fell back and reached for his cap to take it off. Even the Leopard himself, who had never been told of the existence of a half-brother, leaped down from Backlash and the two watchers at the meadow fence could almost hear the wheels grinding in Axel's brain.

"Crispin, did you know there was a half-brother?"

"Yes. Hush."

The Leopard and the Guardian of the Ford stood facing one another in silence until the Leopard said quietly, "You have two of my horses in your meadow."

The other raised his eyebrows in surprise and looked over. "I see only two horses promised to me by the Abbot of Harklinden."

"You perhaps have not heard that the abbey and forest have been placed under a ban, the entire holding to be administered by the Archduke of Tryce."

"On the contrary, I heard of the ban from the abbot himself the day before it was proclaimed. He told me that he would find some way of getting the horses to me."

At this Crispin drew in his breath and glanced at Sarah. He felt as though someone was looking over his shoulder and he had no idea who.

"I have been following your tracks all night, from the abbey stable to your meadow. Those two horses were in the stable when we arrived last night. They were not there an hour or so later. How can you deny absconding with abbey property?"

"I have been in the inn all night," Riverford answered steadily, "sitting up with three travelers. How these horses got here, I have no idea, but I welcome them gladly. And have no intention of letting them go."

"But, you see, I am the Archduke." Axel, somewhat melodramatically, pushed his hood all the way back and opened his cloak. "Surely I may claim what is mine in my own Archduchy?"

"As you must realize, your Grace," (said with no deference whatever) "your jurisdiction does not extend to this side of the river. The land on this side of the ford belongs to me. When the property was given to my mother, I and my heirs were designated Guardians of the Ford, so long as we should last."

"Designated? Given? By whom?"

"Surely, your Grace, there is no need for you to ask."

Crispin was afraid that the Leopard would strike Riverford across the face with his crop, but Axel had immense self-control when he thought it would get him anywhere. Rarely did he have to use it, for bullying was usually easier and quicker. Now the two men regarded each other in silence.

"What you say is true," the Archduke said almost pleasantly. "There is no need to ask." There was silence again, then, "I and some friends of mine would like to pass through the ford this evening. Keep the horses. Let them be an earnest of my regard."

"The horses I intend to keep, now that they are in my meadow. Passage of the ford is another matter."

"Another matter?"

"Another matter, your Grace. You see, Abbot Blaise warned me explicitly against letting you and your friends cross the ford. I promised to heed his warning and bend every effort to forbid your crossing."

"But we are across already."

"Very true, but now you have no destination other than The Legendary Boar. It is only when you have a destination beyond, that I am to forbid your crossing."

"If you can."

But that was a mistake. It was a threat, and Axel knew immediately that he had miscued, and tried to cover his mistake by saying, "If you can see your way to permitting me to cross, I would be eternally grateful. May I assume," trying to change the subject, "that the abbot and monks of Harklinden left the forest over this ford?"

"If I can hold the ford against force, I most certainly will try. If not, I suppose we shall both suffer the consequences. As for the abbot and the monks, no one has crossed the ford, in either direction, for some weeks. Excepting the Abbot, to talk to me, and those horses, and yourselves. No one."

"Well then," said the Leopard, purring almost pleasantly, "since they have not left this way, we won't need to use your ford, will we?" He smiled, he actually smiled at his half-brother, as a snake before it strikes, but the other looked impassively back. "Come then, Ulf, Dorn, let us return to the abbey. By means of the ford. With your permission." He nodded benignly to Riverford but did not wait for confirmation. He sprang nimbly onto Backlash and clattered down into the water, followed by his men.

"Holy casmittima!" Crispin turned to Sarah, "I wouldn't trust that man as far as I could throw him."

"Riverford certainly won't," she returned, "and I'd put my money on him any day."

A handsome woman, just passed middle-age, had come out of the inn as soon as the three riders disappeared into the forest. She had the same white streak in her dark hair that Crispin knew from his Uncle Fritz.

"What do you think he'll do?" the woman asked her son, nodding in the direction of the forest.

"Round up his so-called 'friends' and try to force the ford."

"What will you do, Frederick?"

"We're a little bit short of friends at the moment, living this secluded life that we do. Travelers who have stopped here are no help. And I've turned back too many poachers to be able to count on the locals. What I *will* do is ride over to Chase Longshanks and let him know what's in the wind. He may be willing to help, since his place is most likely their destination."

By this time an ostler had appeared from the barn, digging sleep from eyes and brushing hay from his clothes. Then, from the inn, came a remarkably pretty younger woman carrying a baby. She came and stood close to her husband and asked, "What was that all about?"

"A family reunion," he said, taking the baby and tossing it up over his head and catching it until it crowed with delight.

A young scullion leaned out of a kitchen window, whistled between his teeth, and pointed at the building to signify that the travelers were up and had begun asking for breakfast. A small girl appeared with a big empty pail and went off to milk the two cows. The ostler scattered some grain for the hens. The rooster crowed a final panegyric; the sun rose; the day had begun.

"I'm ready for bed," said Crispin.

"Cheer up. When we get back it will only be a second after we left. Hand me the umbrella, will you please?"

NINE

TARQUIN TAKES OFF

The stars swung through the heavens while Crispin slept. Or so it seemed. The cosmic winds blew the Pleiades into full bloom; the moon waxed and waned and waxed again; the months blew off the calendar one by one as they used to do in movies which you have never seen. Or so it seemed as the boy plunged down into the darkling sea-stream, down toward the hand, toward the word that continually unravels chaos. In those depths sleep did its work and then, like a springtime salmon, he headed home. When he finally broke the surface of sleep he found someone sitting by his bedside.

"Hello, Yettie. What are you doing here?"

"Well, young man, you've been asleep so long your mother was worried and asked me to call the minute you woke up. She and your father are at a dinner. Which reminds me, you've missed all three meals. Which one would you like to start with? Breakfast, lunch or dinner?"

"Holy casmittima! What day is it?" He threw off the sheet and bounded out of bed, all in one movement, and went to the window. Outside the world was at breathless dusk, growing neither lighter nor darker. A white moon had mostly turned its other cheek so that only the slenderest curve was visible.

"It's Saturday, if you must know, and not too much left of that. About 8:30. You put on your bathrobe and slippers and straighten your hair while I call your mother. Then we'll see what we can do for you in the kitchen." She was at the door but stopped before she went out. "Your brother's been looking for you."

Crispin went into the bathroom, banged on the other door and walked in, but Tarquin was not there. He drew water in the basin, used the washcloth on his face, ran a comb through his hair until the snarls came out. He clappered down the tower stairs in slippers and bathrobe with that wonderful feeling of being able to scuff his heels without being taken to task for it.

He was just finishing an extra piece of bread and gravy when Tarquin walked in looking hot and sticky. "Hey, bread and gravy! Let's have some," and, using his foot, hiked up the kitchen stool to the table.

Henriette was sitting keeping Crispin company at the table. "You just finished your dinner a short time ago. You can't possibly be hungry again."

"Dinner was *hours* ago; it's almost dark out."

"And you have no idea how to ask for things. You don't need something to eat, you need a bath."

"May I please have some bread and gravy, Yettie? I promise to take a bath without any coaxing."

"Don't be too nice about it or I'll start to worry," said she, getting up. "I'll have to put the heat on under the gravy again but it'll only take a minute. Meanwhile, wash your hands, if you don't mind."

Tarquin knew that last bit meant "or else," but he got up on the stool and leaned across the table to Crispin. "We have to have a council of war," he mouthed silently.

His brother's eyes widened and he mouthed back, "Why?"

"It's Chase Longshanks. I don't think . . . "

"I don't hear you washing your hands," Yettie said with her back turned, stirring the gravy.

"Yes mam, right away. . . . he's taking this attack seriously." He washed his hands quickly at the kitchen sink, dried them even more quickly, but as he came back to the table Yettie was setting down his plate of bread and gravy, his knife, fork and napkin. She put a cup of chocolate pudding and a spoon in front of Crispin and took away his empty plate. Then she sat down again in her original place, took out her knitting, settled her spectacles on her nose, and said, "I know you boys have important things to talk about so pay no attention to me."

The younger boy found it difficult to give his complete attention to the pudding. Where had Tarquin been and what had he found out? And what was the matter with Chase? He *must* know the Leopard well enough not to trust him. What advice had he been given? And how did he get it? From whom? This brought the boy back to his original question: What had his brother been up to while he slept? He finished his pudding and looked up at Tarquin. He was concentrating mightily on his bread and gravy, with a slight scowl of impatience across his brow.

Crispin finished his glass of milk and asked out loud, "What have you been doing all day?"

"Oh, nothing much. Staying out of people's hair. I went fishing earlier today; that was pretty interesting."

Crispin knew that his brother was an avid fisherman; he also knew that he was not talking about fishing. He asked, "Did you catch anything?"

"One big one that got away from me and one I had to throw back."

"If you boys have finished, just leave the things on the drain board. Tarquin, you are headed for the tub. I want to hear that bath water running within the next few minutes and I want you in it. Please don't leave a ring. I'll be up later to check. Crispin, if you think you can sleep some more, go to bed. If not, you may read until your eyes get heavy. Then turn out the light." She looked at them over the top of her glasses with a "no-nonsense" look.

The two did as directed, thanked Yettie for the food, and left.

"Leave the door open behind you," she said as they went out, "and leave your doors open upstairs." There had been pillow fights and other more serious commotions in the past and Henriette wanted to nip trouble before it flowered.

Tarquin talked while getting ready to take his bath. He disappeared into the bath once to start the water running and to check the temperature. While Crispin listened he roamed up and down the room, picking things up and looking at them without seeing them, then setting them down again and moving on.

"Remember what you said about getting Chase's reaction to the menace? Well, I waited and waited for you to wake up and when you didn't ... I thought I'd better go myself so I did. I wound up back in the library where we were before but under the table this time, which is where I stashed the umbrella because I remembered what you said about being able to see it. There was this really tall guy sitting on the edge of the table so I knew he must be Longshanks and then somebody opened the door and said, 'Riverford to see you, sir.' He said, 'Show him in ...' some name I didn't catch, and in walks Frederick. So he tells Chase everything you saw at the ford and Chase starts to laugh. Honest. He laughed and laughed as though it were the biggest joke in the world and says, 'Finally, a visit from the Archduke. I have been expecting him.' I had crawled out from the other end of the table and Mr. Riverford looked as though he was getting a little hot under the collar. But then Chase said ... let's see ... ah! 'Now, Riverford, you can't possibly stop the Leopard at the ford, not with your resources. It would be foolish of you to try. So you keep everybody indoors and let them sail merrily through.' The bathwater!"

Tarquin dove for the bathroom and turned off the water which had already reached the emergency outlet. Then he reached down to pull the rubber plug and yelled, "Ouch! Damnation!"

"Why didn't you remind me about the water?" he asked, coming out and sitting down on the edge of his bed. "I'll have to let it cool down. I can't even reach the plug. Where was I?"

"Chase was telling Frederick Riverford that he should let them through the ford."

"Yeah, well, then Frederick was telling *him* about how Abbot Blaise warned him not to let them through and that made Chase smile again and he says, 'The Leopard and his men will be more than welcome at Longshanks Hall. I owe him something anyway.' 'But *my* duty is to keep the ford,' says Frederick, and they argue that back and forth for a bit until finally Chase says, 'I'll tell you what. If you think of something really surprising for my friend Axel on his way back, you go right ahead. Like dessert. But I don't think it will be necessary, we will be such good friends by that time.' And that was about it. I'd better go take my bath before Yettie barges in and catches me in my altogether."

"But what about the council of war?"

"It'll have to wait."

Back in his room Crispin turned on the light next to his bed and seated himself on the edge of the bed. He kicked off his slippers, made a prop out of the pillows and stretched out to think, with his head and shoulders propped up and his hands folded on his stomach. To him there didn't seem to be anything wrong with Chase. What he had said was pretty much what anybody would have said who was well-prepared with a surprise reception for the Archduke's attack. And he admired Chase for trying to keep Frederick Riverford out of it. The Guardian of the Ford, with his little family and household, did not need an enemy of the caliber of the Archduke, not even when, and *if*, assisted by the Abbot of Harklinden.

But he was not sure he liked the fact that Tarquin had used the umbrella on his own hook, without consulting him first. *He* had been entrusted with it, and he felt that he was responsible for its use; that, plus a certain possessiveness. It was a very powerful tool and that was doubly important to a small boy who had barely begun to sprout.

He sat up, swung his legs over and dropped into his slippers. But before he could get to his closet Henriette sailed through the doorway. She rapped on the bathroom door and said, "Hurry up in there," then she grabbed him by both shoulders, turned him around and pushed him toward the bed. "Where do you think you're going?"

"I was just going to hunt for something in the closet, Yettie. It'll only take a split second."

"Tomorrow. If it's there it'll keep. If not, you won't find it tonight. Now: bed. I want you both asleep before your parents get home." She raised her voice, "Did you hear that in there?"

The bathroom door opened and Tarquin stood there in his pajamas. He held the umbrella in his hand. "Yes, Yettie, I heard. I just want to put this back where it belongs. I borrowed it."

"I'll take that; you go to bed. I can't imagine what you were doing with an umbrella anyway. Off you go!" She took it from Tarquin, who had the good sense to disappear. She closed the door behind him and hung the umbrella on the glass door knob of Crispin's closet. "Now," she said as the boy finally got into bed, "if your book doesn't put you to sleep, turn off the light and count sheep. And don't go next door."

She went out and passed along the hall to check on his brother. All was dark and quiet in there. Then she looked in on the baby, Justin; she re-passed Crispin's door, only glancing in to make sure he was still in bed, and went downstairs.

Softly the bathroom door opened. "Turn out your light."...a stage whisper from Tarquin. Crispin reached out and pulled the beaded chain, being careful not to look fully into the light. By the time his eyes adjusted to the dark, his brother was sitting at the foot of his bed.

"We've got to have a council of war, and soon," said his brother.

"Yes, why? I thought Chase Longshanks had taken care of everything."

"You really think he's taking this attack seriously?"

"Sure. He knows the Leopard better than we do. It's a surprise party for a surprise attack."

"But that still leaves quadruple-great Uncle Fritz, or whatever relation he is. He's bound to try something."

"Yes, I think so too. I'll bet he doesn't like the Leopard pushing him around. What do you think he'll do?"

"I don't know. That's why we need a council, to figure out how we can help him get the better of the Leopard and his gang."

It was becoming clear to Crispin that his brother was spoiling for a fight of some kind, probably of *any* kind. Was there really anything they could do to aid Frederick Riverford? Sarah might be able to suggest something although she knew Longshanks Hall better than The Legendary Boar. And Blight. He understood everything. He would have to contact Blight.

"About the council: when?"

"I thought tomorrow after Sunday dinner," said Tarquin. "That'll give us most of the afternoon."

"I'm not sure I can get word to Blight by then; or whether he'll be able to make it."

Just then the reflection of automobile head lamps swung around the room and the humming sound of the engine followed.

"Here they are." And Tarquin disappeared through the bathroom into his own room. Crispin unfolded his pillows and restacked them. He dropped his head into the pillows and closed his eyes; he failed to hear his father driving off, taking Henriette home, or his mother quietly closing his bedroom door.

TEN

A SURPRISE IN THE MAKING

Behind him, as he rode away, Riverford heard the stable bell at Longshanks Hall ringing insistently. Chase was summoning a meeting of the few retainers he had, and the tenants, if they could hear the bell. All-told, there were eight retainers; a cook and two others who worked inside, and the five, along with Chase himself, who worked the stables and the huge farm. The wives of those retainers who were married also did service. All admired Chase because he worked hard, was honest, and looked after them. Together they struggled to crawl out from under the load of Axel's debts that went with what had been Trycemeadows.

They came together in the hall along with a few of the nearest tenants who had heard the bell and came jogging in on their great farm horses.

"My friends," Chase spoke to them earnestly, "soon we will be receiving a visit from the Archduke of Tryce and a group of his friends and their roughnecks. It may be tonight. I hope not because that would not give us much time to prepare a fitting reception." This caused a ripple of knowing chuckles. "But it probably will. What have they got in their hearts? Nothing good. Destruction certainly, as much as possible and burning. Most likely theft of horses and cattle, and, who knows, perhaps even killing. Now friends, you know my house is vulnerable. The moat was filled in quite a few years ago, and the drawbridge dismantled. So we can be attacked from any or all sides."

"Which way will they come?" asked one.

"Not from Shanksmare, I think, because they would have to use the ferry and that takes only one horse at a time. However, should they send someone that way, or a few of them, the ferryman will give us warning, will he?"

"As sure as I'm standin' here, he will," said the man who had asked the question.

"Thanks Ned, that's helpful. You will put him wise, will you?"

"Sure thing."

"And they won't be coming from Shipman's Brink because there's no ferry there at all. That leaves the ford. The track from the ford is wide open. It's a distance but it's almost as plain as the road through the Brink. If they get close enough to the house they will undoubtedly use fire. We will have to fight that with water. What we need are the biggest vats and cauldrons we can find placed up on the roof-walks. Then a bucket brigade to fill them. Women and children can help there. The stone and slate won't burn; it's the timbering they'll go for, and any open window. Steven Nyal, may I put you in charge of that?"

"Anything you say," Steven beamed.

"Ned, you slope off to the ferryman, but come straight back and lend a hand wherever you're needed. Rob, you and your son Jim saddle up and ride the track with me and we'll see if there's some way of keeping this gang at a distance. What have I overlooked?"

"Should there be someone at the bell rope to ring a warning when they're on their way?" asked Steven Nyal.

"A good suggestion. Jim, what about your sister, May? She could hang on that bell, could she?"

"Yes sir. She'd love to," said young Jim. "She's been dying to ring it ever since she was tall enough to reach."

"Good. Anything else?" Silence. "Then let's get about it."

Then what a hoisting there was of enormous iron, bronze, and copper cauldrons and vats onto the roofs of Longshanks Hall. The kitchens were quite emptied out, while buckets and pails of water were passed hand to hand up makeshift ladders or carried up interior stairs to attics, passed out of windows onto the leads and so on upward.

Meanwhile, Chase, Rob, and young Jim galloped out of the stables and took the track toward the ford. They came down over the lip of the bowl and thundered over the bridge across the deep, swift stream flowing toward Shipman's Brink. Then they slowed down and looked closely at every turning for some place to ambush, some place that could be held by a few against many. Not much presented itself; the ground was mostly level and the track unfortunately straight, although there *were* places where the woods on both sides crowded the track between them.

More than halfway to the Ford the three turned back, Chase somewhat disconsolately and deep in thought. Young Jim got his father's attention and Rob pulled up next to Chase. "Excuse me, sir, but the boy has an idea." The three halted in the track and Chase smiled encouragingly at the boy.

"Well, sir, . . . I just thought . . . it's true you don't have a drawbridge, or a moat, but you *do* have a bridge, and I thought . . . you see . . . ?"

"I do see. Now. It's the *obvious* things that we never see. Jim, thank you. You have done a great service, I think, and I won't forget it."

He wheeled his great red horse around and said over his shoulder, "Rob, get three other men who are clever with their hands and meet me at the bridge in about half an hour." Then he struck off across country in the direction of Shanksmare, going at a thundering pace, as fast as Vortex could carry him, which was very fast indeed.

The only carpenter in Shanksmare kept his little shop at the end of a short side street. Anything that needed doing in wood, he did. The stonemason did most of the rest.

Chase swung down off the horse; he picked his way through the wood yard hoping that the carpenter would not be away somewhere on a job. But the doors to the shop were closed and bolted from the inside. He knocked gingerly on the door that led up to the room above. No answer. He stepped back and looked up at the little dormer opening on the yard. It too was shut, giving no evidence of life within. He tried a shout. "Able!" No response. He tried to think of any building going on in the neighborhood that he had heard about. Perhaps he should try the local tavern? He turned away perplexed.

In the last house on the street he noticed a curtain fall back over a window. A moment later the street door opened and a woman came out. "Excuse me, squire," she said, "but carpenter, he gone away in a big hurry."

"Do you have any idea where he went?"

"Well, he just about heard your bell ringin' and ringin'. Didn't hear it myself, (mind, I was inside), until he give me a shout as he went by. He brought out ol' Goldenrod and jogged off as fast as that nag'll do. Surprised you didn't meet him on the way down."

"Oh wouldn't you know. No, I came across country."

"Well, you may catch him up yet. Ol' Goldenrod, she don't go too fast. Strong, she is, but not fast. No trouble I hope?"

Chase Longshanks was also a popular man in Shanksmare. Anyone would have been an improvement over Axel Tryce, and the villagers hoped for good things from him when he cleared off his burden of debt. Now he was already in the saddle, steadying Vortex who sensed the urgency of the moment. But he paused to thank the woman and explain about the Archduke of Tryce and his confederates.

"He won't get very far provided I can track down Able Morhaus and get his assistance," said Chase. "Say a prayer that everything turns out well, please." Then Vortex took over. He let the horse

A Surprise In The Making

go at its own pace, feeling that was the best way to save both horse and time.

As they trotted up over the edge of the vale Chase paused and looked about. The manor sat serene in the center of its green bowl filled with October sunlight, invisible to anyone just a short distance down the outside slope. He had grown to love this place, more and more as he invested his life and energies to make it truly his own. That he would defend it with that same energy and life was beyond question.

From where he sat he could see right over the roofs of the Hall and over the stables to the gardens beyond. They, alas, were getting increasingly overgrown with bindweed and nettles. Some day they too would be scoured clean when there would be, perhaps, a wife to oversee the scouring. He stroked and patted his horse and, yes, there was Goldenrod tethered outside his door. So they jogged down.

Able Morhaus turned out to be a technician as well as a carpenter. When Chase brought him down to the bridge he understood its construction at a glance. When Chase explained what he wanted done with the bridge, he sucked his teeth and squinted his eyes. "Weeell . . . we can do that. Take a little time but . . . yes, we can do that. Tools?"

"We have a workshop of tools at the Hall. Use any, or all if necessary. And here are four handy men to assist. It is very important that this be done before nightfall. If you need more men I will supply until we run out. Is that possible?"

"Before nightfall? Yeeess . . . or maybe just after."

They fell to. Riders dashed to the Hall and came back with saws and mallets, bit, braces, wooden pegs, rope and heavy twine. The men clambered down both sides of the steep banks. Since the stream was too deep, wide, and swift to be waded or easily swum, they fixed a rope swing by which tools could be passed quickly back and forth. When necessary, the men used the swing as well, occasionally getting a dunking to the delight of their fellows. Ropes had to be swung over high tree branches (young Jim scampered up and down with ease) with all the men dragging at one end while pieces were removed, refitted, and replaced. Despite wise remarks and good-natured laughter, the men worked seriously and carefully, doing exactly as they were told.

Through the afternoon Able Morhaus walked back and forth on the bridge, directing and advising. Occasionally he climbed down under the bridge himself with his measure and his eye. Sometimes he was accompanied by agile Jim to hold his tools while he tapped and measured or sawed a delicate bit himself.

Evening came. Darkness gradually filled in between the trees and then filled up the meadows and fields. The men withdrew. Anyone riding over the bridge would not have noticed a difference.

ELEVEN

THE SHORT CUT

Crispin sat at the dining room table with a book open in front of him. He and his family had been to Mass at St. Barnabas in West Waffle, the village on the other side of the hill; they had had Sunday breakfast, a more or less cooperative effort since Henriette would not be in until later in the morning. The boy had filled milk and cream pitchers, helped set the table, and started making toast. He had found time to stash a book underneath his chair; he was not permitted to bring a book to family meals. Now everyone else had left the table, the windows onto the lawn were wide open behind him, and deep June poured down out of the skies onto the entire countryside. Mrs. Agincroft passed the door with the baby in her arms and glanced in. He sat with his elbow on the table and his fist holding up his head. For once in his life he was not reading the book open in front of him.

Then Baby Justin came through the door in his diapers and nothing else. He was walking without help these days and could cover an amazing amount of floor in a very short time.

"Hi! Justin Baby Bubbles! Come see your brother." And Crispin leaned down and held out his arms. "Watch your head!" But the baby still fit under the table and trotted gleefully into the waiting arms. "Little Fatso, you're getting awfully heavy." And he hauled the baby into his lap. Then he saw that his mother had come in quietly and was sitting across the table from him.

"How is my middle son?" she asked.

"Oh I'm OK." One seldom knew just what parents had in mind when they asked that question. He handed Justin a spoon and the baby used it to bang a tattoo on the open book.

"You barely said a word during breakfast; you look . . . preoccupied. And you weren't reading your book when I passed the door. Don't you think you can tell me? It's something more than just going to your Uncle's for a few days?"

Crispin put his head down and made vulgar noises on the baby's bare shoulder with his mouth. This was the mother who had surprised him by her knowledge of the forest. That was before he had learned that she was a daughter and a sister of the Guardian of the Ford. Looking back, he felt sure that she had recognized the umbrella that day in the kitchen when he had been trying to conceal it behind his back and she had asked to see it. But even afterwards, after the lifting of the ban, she had never mentioned it to him. Now he looked up at his mother and said, "You know about the umbrella."

"Ah, the umbrella." She raised her eyebrows, paused, then let them back down. "Yes. I know about the umbrella."

"Do you know how it works? Did you ever use it?"

"Yes, I know how it works and, yes, I have used it. You are using it?"

"Yes."

"I thought so. When you slept all day Friday that was the first thing that crossed my mind."

"But you stopped."

"Yes, I stopped. And I suppose you will, too. Sooner or later you will have to choose, as I did."

"Choose? I don't understand. Choose what?"

"Whether you are going to live in the present or in the past."

"Did you have to choose?"

"Yes. I chose the present, as must be obvious, and have your father, Tarquin, you and Justin as my reward."

"But I'm in the middle of something right now, with Tarquin and Sarah Falkrest."

"And the Leopard of Tryce?"

He glanced at his mother. She always seemed to be a half-step in front of him, which was pretty unnerving. Now Justin had grown tired of the spoon and begun to squirm and tried to stand up and put his fingers in his brother's eyes, so Crispin set him down on the floor and looked back at his mother.

"What makes you think that?" he asked.

"You lifted the ban . . ."

Crispin waited. He was learning very quickly when to speak and when to hold off and see what developed.

" . . . and the Leopard is, or *was*, a very interesting character. Not likable but fascinating in his way. We tend to find evil more interesting than good, anyway."

"Why?"

"Oh, dear. Why? Oh no you don't!" She scooped up Justin as he was heading for the door and began putting him into his sun suit. "Maybe it's because there wouldn't be any stories without it. Hold still you little monkey while I do these buttons . . . there. Now run along and find your father or your eldest brother and ask them to play."

Justin headed for the pantry but once again he was headed off by Mrs. Agincroft, who got him started into the living room where his father was deep into the Sunday papers. Then she came and sat down again.

"How long do you want to stay at your Uncle Fritz's?"

"Just for a day or two. There's a short cut from the abbey to the ford and Greyfell is going to have his grandson teach it to me."

"Is there a short cut indeed? He never told me that."

"He might not have told me, but Blight found it on an old Harklinden map. So I asked him about it."

"I suppose it stands to reason that there would be. Learn it and you can show it to me some day. If we go right after dinner we can drop you and be back before it gets too late. Go upstairs and take off your good clothes; pack up what you need in your knapsack – that should be enough – and go outside and get some sunshine. I'll call my brother to give him advance warning."

* * *

The boy led Vortex out of the stable to the mounting block. His uncle watched from the stone platform above. "What time will you be back?" he asked. "For lunch?"

"I'm hoping Blight will be able to give me something. And another apple for my buddy here," and he patted the horse on the neck; then he sprang lightly into the saddle from the top of the block. To Vortex he had explained all about Torfell the young wolf while the horse was munching his apple in the stable. So that was all right. But his uncle surprised him when he said, "There was a wolf howling last night. Was that for your arrival?"

"I think maybe it was."

"There's one sitting on that balding dome over there. He was there when I first looked out." He pointed with a thrust of his chin to a great, bare forehead of rock that stuck out slightly from the others in the bank across the river.

Crispin looked over, shading his eyes from the morning sun and, sure enough, there was a young wolf sitting on the top of the rock and looking right at him. Even at that distance he could feel the yellow eyes looking right into him. It was a piercing gaze not unlike his Uncle Fritz's except that his uncle's eyes were so dark blue they were almost black.

"Holy casmittima, I wish I'd known, I would have gotten up earlier. Come on, Vortex, I think we're late."

"He will stay 'til you come."

The horse trotted down into the ford and sent showers of crystals into the morning air. The minute the two began to move the wolf disappeared from its lookout. As they came up the gentle slope from the water, there was the wolf, standing in the middle of the track. The boy put his left hand into the front of his shirt and stuck a finger through the Ring of Harklinden. Vortex came to a halt and stood with neck arched, unmoving.

"It is not often that I find a wolf in my path," said the boy.

"It is not often that I find a young man and a horse in mine," said the wolf. "Among my family I am known as Torfell, but my real name is something quite other."

Then the horse said, "They have given me the name Vortex, but my real name is also something quite other."

"My name is Crispin Timothy Eilif Agincroft; it is the only name I have."

"So you are already known among my family and clan. I am pleased and proud to meet you, Crispin Timothy Eilif Agincroft. My grandfather speaks very highly of you. He has asked me to guide you over the short cut. Once you get into it, it's pretty plain; finding it in the first place is what baffles."

Torfell turned about and trotted a few paces down the broad track. Just where it turned sharply east a great rock had split into halves and a huge evergreen had grown up in the split, its branches touching their fringe to the dust of the track. The rock itself was part of a whole shelf of stone that formed a high wall along the west side of the track. The wolf paused just opposite the tree.

"A man or a boy on a horse," he said, "can push their way past the trunk of this tree into the split, which widens a little on the other side. At the end, immediately to the left, there is another split at right angles. Anyone looking in past the tree would not see the second split; the tree continually casts a shadow that makes it invisible. We will make the turn into the second split, make another to the right that takes us up a sloping path to the top of this wall. Follow me."

Crispin crouched down against his horse's neck as Vortex pushed into the split past the evergreen trunk. For the horse and rider it was something like going into the starting gate at a race track, and Vortex gave a distasteful snort but followed the wolf through the zigzag cut, and in a moment or two they were rising through great trees up a path almost invisible because so long out of use.

Again the wolf paused and looked back. "A morning's run may be in order. The trail is so straight it is difficult to go wrong but I will keep ahead of you if I can." So off they went at a wild gallop. The trail rose so gently that one was scarcely aware that it was doing it. The hooves of Vortex made hardly a sound as they passed over pine needles, then exploded into a drum-roll across flat rock or harder ground exposed to the sun. A stream crossed their track, dropping from lip to lip of shelving stone, and they stopped to drink. The horse got down on his knees so that the boy could also dismount and drink, plunging his face right into a swirling pool, and telling Vortex what an intelligent, clever horse he was before getting back into the saddle.

Almost at the top of everything, where Crispin could see out over rolling waves of forest, darkened here and there by fleeting cloud shadow, at the top of a knoll of grass, was one of the vanished monks' cells. Its back stood against the final outcropping of rock which shielded it, somewhat, from the west winds. A squat, stone cabin it was, with a low chimney almost as big as itself. The door had fallen in long ago but out of the opening tumbled a pack of noisy wolf cubs that gave Vortex second thoughts about this entire excursion.

Torfell, after driving them back with good-natured barks and nips, turned apologetically to horse and rider. "This used to be the 'den' of the monks who looked after our clan. Even after all this time their reputation lives with us as wise and kindly men, speaking our tongue, and knowing our ways as well as we know them ourselves. But when the ban fell, all that knowledge was lost, except the little that may have found its way into books. There is a spring just a bit further along from which they drew their water. We, too, can drink at Wolfspring. Troop dismissed!" he barked at the little pack, then turned and trotted down the trail, which also began its long descent, broken occasionally by stretches that rolled over low ridges or dipped through water courses.

Further along, they were walking through a long glade where great beeches had made room for themselves, keeping other trees at the very end of their unbelievably long branches. No undergrowth grew in the dense shade of these enormous trees, just wispy green grass with the thread of trail running straight as though drawn with a ruler. "Torfell," said Crispin. The wolf, no longer out in front, was walking along almost under the boy's stirrup. "Torfell, what was it like living under the ban?"

There was silence. They paced along into sunlight and shadow. Then the wolf spoke. "Like holding your breath for days without end. Like living under these trees in perpetual shade. We spoke mostly in whispers and looked over our shoulders, because after the killing of the Leopard so long ago, when everyone thought things would get better, they got worse. Even in death he roamed the forest like one possessed and we were terrified of running into him. You see, when he couldn't find his brother or any of the monks, he thought they had turned themselves into wolves. He was determined to drive us out."

"I had no idea it was so bad, Torfell. I'm sorry I brought it up. But maybe you can tell me why I find the Leopard so interesting."

"Do you?" Torfell looked up at the boy with puzzled curiosity. "I don't. Not at all. Do you, Vortex?"

"No, not I."

"But I do. And my brother is fascinated, I think."

"Perhaps that is because you recognize a fellow-feeling," said the wolf hesitantly.

"Stop!" Crispin remembered the one time he had encountered the Leopard face to face in the dark barn at Longshanks. At that time he had, against his will, looked into the Leopard's eyes and seen there what, even at his age, he had recognized as death. Now he freed his feet from the stirrups, swung a leg over and dropped to the ground. Then he ran around in front of the horse and looked up into his great brown eyes and into the yellow eyes of the wolf.

"Vortex, my friend; Torfell – fellow-feeling! Do you really believe I could become like that?" He was troubled and hurt and looked angrily at both.

"To us, human beings are more mystery than anything," Vortex said.

Torfell said, "We are both young and know very different things. Perhaps we can learn from each other."

"I hope so."

"Already you are a hero to me and my clan."

Once again the horse slowly folded its legs and got down on it knees. He said, "Crispin, get up on my back and I will carry you."

"And I will guide you as far as I can," said the wolf.

And away they went like the wind.

*　*　*

Frederick Riverford, Blight, and Crispin were eating dinner at a small table in the large inn kitchen. With some pride, the boy had brought back Blight on Nightmare, over the sort cut which halved the time to go from Abbey to Ford. When, earlier, Torfell led had him back down to the main track, not far from the Abbey itself, he had said, "You will travel the cut with ease from now on. I shall look forward to seeing you again. Until next time."

"Wait! How will I let you know?"

"The forest is very, very large; it is also very small, and full of eyes and ears. Just bark." Within seconds the young wolf had disappeared back up the cut.

"I never thought I'd meet a wolf I liked," Vortex said, shaking his head.

Now the boy was enjoying dinner because he had built up a terrific appetite during the day. Uncle Fritz mostly did his own cooking. It was simple and tasty but Crispin secretly missed the glutinous desserts that Yettie concocted. A young man who bicycled in from Cutting Edge was looking after the regulars in the tap room, so both his uncle and Blight were relaxed and talkative.

From the short cut, which Crispin told about, they had gone on to talk about "Forest Management" and how the monks lived out the Rule of Harklinden, coming in to the abbey once a week on Sundays to sing in choir, celebrate a community Mass, and share a dinner and recreation. The other six days they lived as hermits, each in his own cell, which were distributed about the forest, like the Wolfspring cell. There they lived, praising God, managing the forest, and making their little vegetable gardens grow. As their numbers increased they also set out, two by two, to new forests and, where possible, began new foundations. Otherwise they set up schools in which they taught what they knew best, forests. Now Uncle Fritz (the new Abbot Frederick), and Blight (his Prior), were looking forward to picking up the pieces as best they could, and recovering the lost art of forest management.

Crispin listened with great interest. The more he discovered of the forest for himself, the more he felt there was to learn and do. He also wanted to ask these two men his question. What Torfell had said about "fellow-feeling" still rankled in his memory. Like the forest, he felt there was a large part of himself still undiscovered -- unknown countries as there were in his school geography book.

He had only to wait, and not too long, before the conversation crossed the trail of the Leopard and his bane. "It's quite remarkable," Blight said, "how one evil man can have such an effect and for so long, and then come back in different ways to . . . what shall I say? 'haunt' us. We don't seem to be able to get rid of him once and for all."

"What makes you think we really want to?" asked the Guardian.

"Uncle Fritz, that's the question I've been waiting to ask," exclaimed Crispin. "Why are we so interested in this wicked man? I asked Mother and I asked Torfell and they both gave me an answer, but . . . they make sense and all, but . . ."

"But they don't answer the question. I'd be interested to know what my sister told you."

"That there wouldn't be any stories without evil."

"That's fair enough. A mother to a young son. That's something to go on. From the Bible right through Homer and Shakespeare and Dickens . . . they've all got it or we wouldn't read them. Or there wouldn't be any stories at all."

"I'd be interested to know what the wolf said," chimed in Blight.

The boy looked from one to the other, these two good men who had become so important in his life, who gave him no signs of faults or failings, how could anyone . . . "He said we recognize a fellow-feeling."

Blight let out his breath like the final air going out of a balloon. "Now how could that young wolf know that?"

"But is he right? He can't be right, can he?"

Uncle Fritz scraped bread crumbs together on the tablecloth with the edge of a knife. Blight slumped back in his chair and drummed his fingers on his chest. The older man spoke first.

"Well, Crispin," he said, "it's not the last word on the subject, but it's close. And it's a true word. Kindred spirits. Kin. The human family. We're all in this together."

The boy, perplexed, looked to the younger man who had shared his quest, been patient and helpful and understanding. Blight had kept him steady when he was going to fly off angrily in some wrong direction. Now he looked at the boy from beneath his eyebrows, then sat up, folded his arms on the table and leaned on them. "You want an answer, don't you? A solution?"

Crispin sat silent for a minute. He felt that he was not going to get a solution, that he would be lucky to get an answer that fit the question. The kitchen clock ticked. Remotely he could hear laughter and talk from the tap room. Finally he said, "Just tell me the last word."

Blight shook his head and smiled. "How do you manage to keep a half-step ahead of me?"

"Family trait," Uncle Fritz murmured.

Crispin waited.

"The *second*-last word is *death*."

"And the last?"

"*Resurrection*."

TWELVE

HEADS TOGETHER

A flashlight swept through the black, and then another. Crispin was running but not fast enough nor far enough. Then in front of him – searchlights sweeping the dark. Where was he? He could not recognize where he was. He *should* be able to. He tried. But he could not. Where? Where *was* he? No! They are not searchlights at all, those seeking, grasping lights are eyes! Eyes looking for him, and he felt their lights pass over his body. Hide! Where? There was no place. Then *run*. But there was no place. It was the great barn. The great stone barn at Longshanks, was it? And the Leopard's eyes were drawing him in, gathering him in. Until . . . he was drawn, irresistibly drawn to those eyes, drawn to the top of a tall tower, in danger of falling, drawn irresistibly over the edge into the glare of those eyes. Then . . . then . . . somewhere a word was spoken. He *knew* it was spoken although he could not hear it. It was a beautiful word. His eyes filled with tears it was so beautiful, and he longed to have it spoken again. He was in a round place. A silo? No, the tower. It was the chapel and he was looking into those eyes which looked so steadily into his. Oh, let him speak that word again.!

   His head was pressed down into his pillow and his cheeks were wet with tears, and his eyes too, as they opened. Above him and from his right the ceiling slanted upwards. Through the open dormer he could hear the continual, comforting rustle of the river over the ford. *Oh, let them speak that word again,* he thought, and tried to plunge back into sleep. But he only heard the loquacious riddle of the ford.

Then it began to rain. On the ceiling, the roof, the slates above his head, like an insistent rolling of timpani. But he was safe and dry and the sound of the rain pouring down opened into profound, shoreless sleep.

* * *

Sarah had cleared a space on the long table in the library, carefully moving aside and stacking some of the ledgers she was working through. Now she sat in her customary place at the head of the table in her wheelchair, her glasses pushed up on her forehead, with Crispin on one side and Tarquin on the other. Blight was sitting further along next to Crispin. They all looked very serious.

"We certainly can't keep them from crossing the ford," Crispin was saying, "that's pretty clear."

"Even if we could, I don't think we should." That was Sarah's opinion.

"Why not?"

"Well, we know that Chase Longshanks is a very capable young man, especially when it comes to defending his own. Since he has prepared a surprise party for the Leopard, I rather think we should let him throw it. I think it will be more effective than anything we could pull off."

"Wouldn't you like to know what he has up his sleeve!" Crispin's eyes sparkled.

"He may just finish them off." Tarquin maintained a colossal dislike of the Leopard which only helped disguise his reluctant fascination.

"I don't think he will do that," Blight put in.

"Why not? I'll bet he could."

"It would just make more trouble for him. The Archduke doesn't have any family left, except the Abbot and the Bishop, Trycewinning, but his three confederates do, rather considerable families. I don't suppose they would take it lying down."

"Revenge. A blood feud. Terrific!" exclaimed Tarquin.

"I think we can count that out as a possibility, can't we?" Blight looked to Sarah.

"As far as I know," she said.

Tarquin, somewhat disappointed, asked, "Well, what then? What's left?"

Crispin said, "What we want to do (I've been thinking about this a lot), what we want to do is something to keep them from ever coming back or getting back at Frederick Riverford and The Legendary Boar."

"That sounds very reasonable to me. What do you have in mind?" Blight asked.

"I haven't been able to think of anything yet," the boy said somewhat lamely. "I was hoping somebody else might. Tarquin or Sarah."

"We could drop out of trees onto their backs. That would scare the pants off them."

"But there are only three of us," Sarah pointed out, "and about fifty of them. And I'm not sure I would want to drop out of a tree, even if I could get up into it in the first place."

The four sat in silence for a minute. Again Tarquin suggested something: "What about the wolves in the forest? Couldn't they do something? Attack them on the way to the ford or on the way back?"

"Torfell has already volunteered their services, but that would mean letting the Leopard and his men back across the ford."

"And I think Frederick Riverford is determined to prevent that, if possible," was Sarah's opinion. "That's where we could do the most good, if we could just think of something."

Tarquin got up from the table and paced over to the windows and then back and over and back.

His brother put his forehead down on his folded arms and tried to imagine the event. Here came the approaching cavalcade, galloping toward the Ford from under the midnight trees. There stood the Guardian of the Ford with one or two others, pitchforks in their hands. Here they come, thundering along the lane in full flight, pursued by Chase and his own retainers -- the rustlers pursued by the sheriff and his deputies, the Sheriff of Nottingham and Guy of Gisborne pursued by Robin Hood and his men – but usually it was the other way around. They come crowding down the dark lane, hell bent for leather – Ichabod Crane pursued by the Headless Horseman ready to throw his burning head. Except that there were no pumpkins this time of year.

The older brother returned to the table with his hands in his pockets, slumped down again in his chair, stretched out his legs, and muttered, "Rats."

"Fireworks!"

"What?"

But Blight got the idea immediately; Sarah caught her breath.

"Fireworks. You know, sky rockets and roman candles. Not up in the air, but *aimed*. Whooosh, bam! They've never seen fireworks," declared Crispin.

Tarquin looked with unbelief at his brother. "That is brilliant. That is absolutely, fabulously brilliant!" And he went into a paroxysm of swooshes and explosions and said, "And whistle bombs too." He lit up from the inside; he glowed with anticipation; he asked, "Where do we get them?"

"Leave that to me," said Blight. "There's a shop in Chewing Cud, and if they don't have them, Tryceholdings certainly will. What sort of range will we need?"

They put their heads together and calculated the distance from the forest across the river, past the inn to the trees on the other side.

Sarah and Blight worked on angles of elevation and approximate carrying power.

"Should they all be coming from the same direction?"

"It would certainly make it a lot easier to coordinate."

"But they would know they were not surrounded."

"A point well-taken. Would it make a difference?"

"We'll need chutes or troughs to lay the sky rockets in for firing."

"Will the umbrella take them or leave them behind?"

They plotted down to details, ironed out wrinkles, foresaw difficulties and shunted them aside. Finally Tarquin clapped Crispin on the back, shook his hand, said (generously), that he had salvaged the entire expedition, and disappeared, leaving the umbrella for his brother. Then the other two said "Goodbye" to Sarah, mounted, and rode back to the ford as directly as possible along the track and path they thought the Leopard and his confederates would take. Both timed the trip, Blight with his wristwatch and Crispin with his grandfather's big pocket watch that had helped him through his quest.

THIRTEEN

RAIN AND MRS, P

Blight knocked together three wooden chutes that could be easily directed and redirected, raised or lowered. These he delivered to the library at Longshanks Hall. They stood on the floor in the bay window, pointing out over the lawn. Tarquin felt that he ought to be present at the purchasing of the fireworks and talked Crispin into coming along.

"But Blight is perfectly capable of getting everything we need."

"He may miss something spectacular. Anyway, he probably won't buy enough."

"Well, we're not fighting a war, you know. It probably won't even be a battle," reasoned the younger boy.

"Then we can have a celebration when it's over."

That did it. Crispin loved fireworks and the thought of a little spectacle at the end did the trick. Furthermore, he did not like to have Blight always spending his own money, so, since neither he nor Tarquin were given allowances, he asked his father for some money.

* * *

Chewing Cud was a market town, but only once a month. The rest of the time it went about its businesses in a sleepy sort of way, looking with mild suspicion at strangers, and taking everyone else for granted. It was used to the Pierce Arrow and Blight, although not to the two boys in the front seat. However, the town had its own share of young boys to keep track of; two more made little difference. The shop they were going to fronted onto the market square, identifying itself with a sign above the door that read simply, P. Larke. The door stood open but a beaded curtain kept the summer flies out. In one corner of the shop window stood a colorful sign that appeared to be the result of a grade-school project. Its letters, spelling out FIREWORKS, were painted vertically on a shirt board amid zigzags of lightning and a burst of gold stars that had been licked and stuck on. The three went in.

Inside, the place smelled faintly of coffee, cheese, bread, or kerosene, depending on where you were standing. The fireworks were in the rear of the shop on a special counter all to themselves. The fire crackers, in paper packages of electric greens, violent blues, and Chinese reds, were arranged according to size and price. The more exotic and expensive sky rockets and Roman candles stuck out of boxes on the shelves behind. A remote-looking woman in an apron, with coat sweater over, waited on them, and put everything in a cardboard box after Blight asked her if she had one. He was very reluctant to use Crispin's money until he realized that it was a matter of justice for the boy. Tarquin, in enthusiastic anticipation of Armageddon, insisted that they spend it all. Not that the sum was all that much, but it proved to be quite enough.

"Celebration?" asked Mrs. P. Larke mildly, as she counted out the few pennies in change.

"An event," put in Blight quickly, before Tarquin could say anything that sounded bloodthirsty.

"Oh, an event. That' nice." She pushed the box towards them across the counter.

To the boys' surprise Blight said, "And I think three ice cream cones are in order, double scoops, please."

No reaction from Mrs. P. Larke except, "Vanilla or chocolate?"

The scoops were big; the ice cream was rich; Blight made them finish before they got back into the Pierce Arrow. The next day Blight delivered the cardboard box to the Longshanks library.

"Fireworks, is it," said McGuiness, peering gimlet-eyed through his glasses into the box. "Mum's the word."

There needed only the event.

* * *

"It's raining," said Crispin.

"No it isn't," insisted his brother.

"Of course it's not raining *now*; it's raining *then*."

"But you're not wet."

"That's because it's not raining now; it's raining then. And very hard, too. It's pouring."

"Thunderation!" exclaimed Tarquin.

The faces around the table looked serious.

"What are we going to do?" asked Sarah.

"Wouldn't you know it would be raining. That spoils everything."

As a test, Crispin had taken one of the chutes under his arm and used the umbrella to go back to the ford before the Leopard and his marauders passed through. He was very glad he had the umbrella above him and put it up all the way until it clicked and the rain pounded on top. Then he looked around. He was standing on a bare rock. It was fairly high above the river, the same out-cropping that he had first seen Torfell lying on. The rain teemed into the river beneath him, erasing every wave and ripple except those at the ford itself. The rain also splattered and bounced off the rock and, in spite of the umbrella, he could feel droplets on his bare legs. He was about to say, "Take me back, please," but stopped himself. Instead, he said, "Rules for using the umbrella: If you want to take it with you, start lowering it first." He did that.

"Take me back, please." Here he was, dry, with the wooden chute still under his arm.

Blight looked thoughtful, Sarah perplexed, and Tarquin irrepressibly glum.

"There's no reason why fireworks should not work in the rain," Blight said, "provided they are kept dry and fired from a dry place. They shoot guns and cannon in the rain and snow, don't they? Of course, our explosives are wrapped in paper, not metal, but we're not shooting them underwater, either. Can it be raining that hard, Crispin?"

"It *is* raining very hard, but it could let up any minute, I suppose. With luck."

Sarah had pressed an electric bell on the table and now McGuiness stuck his head unceremoniously through the door and asked, "What'll you have?"

"Mac, are there any umbrellas left around this place? Or did they all go in the auction?"

"I think I can find you three, Miss. Does it look like rain?"

"Would you round them up and bring them here, please, like a good boy?"

"I will, in spite of the lip." He shut the door with a snap.

"Mac, bless his heart, gives lip but doesn't *take* it too well. However, he keeps track of everything around here better than either Dads or I. Now, there are four of us and there will be four umbrellas, if they all work. But we shouldn't need all four – just two people to hold them up and two to ignite. Maybe a third over the carton to keep that dry. What about slickers to keep out the damp?"

"We never figured rain into our calculations. I'm afraid we are all unprepared," said Blight.

"Well, let's see what Mac has to say. He'll grouse and complain, but he loves a challenge. If there's anything helpful, we'll get it."

The door opened and McGuiness came in width three dusty umbrellas under his arm. "Behind those sliding panels at the front door, they were. Just as I thought."

"Rain gear, Mac. We could also use some rain gear. Slickers or raincoats. Can you conjure any from your bag of tricks? It would be very helpful."

"Need they fit?" he asked, looking around at the four at the table.

"Better too big than too small," Sarah said. "Just drop those on the end of the table."

McGuiness did that, creating a small cloud of dust and brushing himself off where the umbrellas had left gray lines on his vest. "Send one of those stalwarts with me to carry the gear, can't you?"

"I'll go!" Tarquin jumped up. Any activity was better than simply waiting around; so he disappeared out the library door in the wake of the faithful family retainer. Blight and Crispin took the umbrellas out onto the lawn, shook the dust out and opened and closed them quickly several times as you do when you are shaking water off. One had a triangular rent in it, so they eliminated that. The other two were satisfactory in spite of a bent rib or two.

"Three of these should do it," said Blight. "We may not be dry ourselves but they should do for the fireworks." They closed them up, went back inside, stood the reject next to the fireplace, and in a minute or two McGuiness was back with Tarquin carrying an armload of tan, cavalry raincoats, five all told.

"Stored in a closet off the tack room," said McGuiness triumphantly. "A bit dusty, but no moths."

"Oh, Mac, you are a peach," the girl said. "Is there one that will fit me?"

They shook them out and held them up as Mac departed. Blight was the easiest to fit and looked very dashing with his closely-trimmed beard and mustache. The girl grinned at him. "With that coat and a monocle you could get by in any officers' mess anywhere. You look to the manner born – more hussar than monk, I would say."

Tarquin, getting big for his age, got one that reached to his ankles but the sleeves were fine when he turned them back once. And Sarah, as near as they could tell by holding one up, would be comfortable and dry. Crispin was out of luck. The best he could do was turn the sleeves back three or four times and hope not to trip on the bottom hem. His brother said, "You could sit on somebody's shoulders and that would make it a fit."

Blight, however, with eyes twinkling, encouraged him. "Don't worry about it, Crispin, you're already taller than when we first met. Just pray you don't have to move in a hurry."

"Well, are we ready to roll now?" Tarquin asked. But a tap came at the door, McGuiness reentered and said, very formally but with a wink, "Excuse me, Miss Sarah, but Mrs. Presskit would like to speak with you." Tarquin suppressed a groan and collapsed back into his chair.

"Mrs. Presskit . . . oh dear . . . well . . . yes. Have her come in, please."

McGuiness opened the door, stepped into the great hall, and said, "Come in, then, Mrs. Presskit."

She looked exactly as she did the last time Crispin had seen her, right down to the big ledger clasped to her bosom. Hair drawn back in a bun, half-glasses held securely in place by an aquiline nose - a pleasant, considerate, helpful-looking woman.

"Miss Falkrest, I am sorry,' she began. "I see I have come at an inopportune moment, but I did want to return the ledger with all the accounts of the auction in it. I have kept it far too long, only because I wanted to double-check and make sure everything was letter-perfect."

"Yes, thank you, Mrs. Presskit, I understand. Most thoughtful of you."

"However, there was one thing that I wanted to bring to your attention and that of Colonel Falkrest. I took the liberty of showing it to *Mr.* Presskit and he said, 'Yes, by all means show it to them, Mrs. Presskit, it is your duty.' I *could* return another day except that I think it quite important. Could we . . . talk, for just a minute?"

Sarah had already begun to turn her wheelchair and get it moving in the direction of the door. "Of course, just step back into the hall, if you would, Mrs. P., we can talk out there." She made an apologetic face at Tarquin as she passed, and rolled out through the door which was closed behind her.

She was gone for what may have been six or eight minutes but which seemed like thirty or forty-five to the two boys, for Crispin, too, had all the impatience of youth except that he kept it bottled-up inside, not wanting to inflict his own temperament on others, or maybe just embarrassed by his brother's example.

Finally the door opened and the girl wheeled herself back into the library with a brightness in her eyes that had not been there when she went out. She said, "Now let us hurry to the rescue of Longshanks Hall and the ford and to dispatch the forces of evil!"

Crispin jumped up in his absurd raincoat, raised his hand and cried, "Down with the Leopard and his desperadoes!" Sarah and Blight gleefully said, "Amen!" whereas Tarquin, cried, "Go team!"

FOURTEEN

TWO SURPRISES

"Suppose they don't come in the rain?" Tarquin asked with a note of reproach in his voice.

The two boys and Blight had each brought a chute and an umbrella with them, and Sarah, because she had to start out still sitting down in her wheelchair, had had the box of fireworks on her lap. She still had it in her arms, but protected underneath her ample raincoat. Blight had used the umbrella only once before and his astonishment had not quite worn off. "Incredible, incredible," he said, but the veterans paid no attention. They huddled under the three umbrellas looking out into the rain in the direction of The Legendary Boar. The inn was showing no lights in its windows.

"They have to come tonight," Crispin reminded his brother. "We said 'the night of the attack' as part of our directions. They may be along any minute."

Then the rain modulated from "monsoon" to "downpour" to "shower," and was giving every indication of going on to "sprinkle," and then 'off'. They waited, and it did.

There was little by way of foliage above them, only a gnarled, old pine tree leaning out over the rock, its few blasted branches offering neither shelter nor shade. From time to time it dripped. But the umbrellas came down and were put out of the way, and the chutes set up. The sky did not clear, and the lop-sided moon, sinking toward the horizon, only occasionally lit up a cloud, like a bad bulb in a lampshade.

"Listen!"

Everything stopped. There it was, the tell-tale jingle and clink of harness, and the thud of hoof-beats that slowed to a walk as they approached the ford. Then they stopped altogether, like the rain, and only a single rider continued. A thin screen of undergrowth separated the four from the track. Through this they could make out the horseman, just a few yards away. He stopped at the top of the gentle slope and looked out. Then he turned back and rejoined the troop.

Tarquin's hand clutched his brother's arm and he whispered, "It's him." But Crispin knew that already. He felt he would recognize the Leopard of Tryce with his back turned and his eyes shut. Thinking about what his mother had said, he wondered, at this particular moment, whether stories were really worth it. Then he heard the troop advancing stealthily two by two, and all four again held their breath. Down the ramp they went and cautiously into the ford. They came up on the other side and passed between the inn and the barn across from it, moving steadily but just beginning to pick up the pace. There was no sound, no movement, no light, no response from the inn.

"There are forty of them." Sarah had counted.

"That's better than fifty," said Blight. Now, look out there; see, that's the range we want, right there as they come out from beneath those trees. There must be about a hundred yards between there and the inn, all open and clear."

"We could pick them off one at a time if we could just have a little practice." Already Tarquin was champing at the bit.

"What do you suppose Chase will do against forty men?"

"Look, there's a light on in the inn."

Not only was there a light burning, but the door opened and two figures crossed to the barn, pausing just long enough to look down the lane where they may have been able to see the last of the disappearing horsemen. Then they went on and opened both sides of the barn door. They dragged out a great hay wagon, empty of hay, into the lane, a third man pushing from behind. They went back in and out came a two-wheeled cart, which they pushed up against the wagon. What with the open doors, the wagon, and the cart, passage of the lane was effectively cut off.

"That's neat," said Blight. "They must be planning on the squeeze-play. The way forward blocked and Chase advancing from behind."

And they can't get around either the inn or the barn because the way looks blocked by other obstacles – walls, fences, hedgerows – 'build a better mousetrap' I always say. Unless they disperse and take to the woods and fields beyond," Sarah added thoughtfully.

Crispin, who had tried to imagine every possibility, said, "I hope one of our sky rockets doesn't go astray and fall into the thatch of the inn."

"Look," Tarquin pointed closer down, "they *must* be concerned about fire; they're getting water from the river."

Except for the baby, the entire family had collected every bucket, pot and pan, and were finishing filling some big wooden barrels that stood next to the inn and the barn.

"What do you suppose Chase has planned for those forty men?" Sarah asked again.

"I don't know, but I think you should go and find out. Just be back in plenty of time. Take Tarquin with you, and Crispin, too. I'll stay here to keep the fireworks dry in case it rains again."

In the dark they could not tell one umbrella from another so they had to try two unsuccessfully before getting the right one. As they arrived near Longshanks Hall, they found themselves perched like fledglings along the limb of a giant oak. Below them was the track from the Ford that, as it approached the Hall, had widened into a broad lane. This lane crossed a substantial wooden bridge that spanned a deep and turbulent stream some ten or fifteen feet below. Across the bridge the land began to rise gently; the Hall was concealed in the bowl on the other side of the rise.

Immediately beneath them a lonely figure sat quietly on his horse. It was Chase. Tarquin, the only one of the three to have seen him so far, recognized him and passed the word along to the other two. But Crispin *did* recognize the great red horse he was riding. He nudged Sarah with his elbow and pointed. The girl nodded and grinned. "Vortex," she said silently. The branch where they were sitting was still wet from the rain and began to soak through their raincoats, which were old and no longer entirely waterproof. Nevertheless, any discomfort they may have felt was soon forgotten.

"Here they come, lads," Chase called softly to unseen assistants concealed somewhere nearby. He rode his horse around behind the trunk of the giant oak and swung himself up into its branches so that the top of his head was just below their dangling feet.

It was clear to Tarquin that Chase was going to drop down on one or two of them and pull them from their horses and bang their heads together. He had half a mind to join in and try the same trick himself. However, as the track widened, the riders behind began to close up so that now they were jogging along towards the bridge four abreast. Because of the high rim of the ground between, the sound of their horses would be inaudible at the Hall; likewise the loud drumming of hooves on the wooden bridge. On they came, picking up more and more speed, and they thundered out over the swift darkness of the swollen stream.

"Now!" shouted Chase at the top of his voice, a sound that re-echoed between the banks below. There was a great knocking and a rending crash and the entire bridge collapsed into the rushing water, bringing down with it the entire company of attackers.

Cries of terrified horses and struggling men arose as they were swept downstream. Chase swung back down onto his horse and started carefully along the bank. "Assist the horses first, and the men if possible, and send them on their way," he called cheerfully.

"Holy casmittima!"

"Wow, what a stunt!" Tarquin practically swooned in an ecstasy of vicarious triumph.

"But hard on the horses." Sarah's first concern.

"And on the non-swimmers," added Crispin. "But I hope we'll still need our fireworks. Do you suppose we will?" He had the umbrella handle around his neck so that he wouldn't drop it. "There's only one way to find out. Let's go."

* * *

One, two, three, they were all back on the rock, letting the older boy make the report. However, he tended to tell most of it with gestures and sound effects so the other two added the explanations.

"Chase Longshanks is clearly no one to monkey-around with," said Blight. "I'm glad he's on our side. Do you think they'll survive, Sarah?"

"I know that stream well," the girl replied. "There's a sand bar and a beach not much further down. It's lovely when the stream is not flooding. I've gone swimming there. If they survive the drop they'll all get washed up there, I would think. Chase may turn them individually over his knees and whale the living daylights out of them."

"Well if that's the case, they may be spoiling for revenge by the time they get here. Every man to his post."

Blight lit two sticks of punk and gave one to each of the boys. They lined up the chutes once again, and again checked the elevations. The girl laid a sky rocket in each chute, making sure the wick was readily available to the smoldering punk. Then Blight gave last minute instructions. "Remember men, you have to anticipate, because it takes a while for the burning wick to reach the explosive charge. Ignite when I say 'Fire!'"

Before very long they could make out some movement among the trees and the faint sounds of hooves jogging in the lane. Then louder.

"Punk ready." The first riders were about to break from the trees.

"Fire!"

The wicks ignited easily with little sparkles which disappeared into the rockets. The riders emerged from the trees. Suddenly 'Wizzsst, wizzsst, wizzsst' the three sky rockets shot up into the dark and Sarah had three more in the chutes. "Fire!" Wizzsst, wizzsst, wizzsst. So the next three were in the air before the first, arching up and over, leaving a trail of fiery spangles, flashed down and burst in the very faces of the leading horsemen. Blossoms and bouquets of green and gold fire exploded. Gas blues and reds followed in quick succession.

"Bullseye!" cried Tarquin. "Quick, a whistle bomb."

Even before the second flight burst, the third was on its way, and then two more rockets and the whistle bomb. This let out a piercing, shrieking scream of a whistle, followed by a BANG that would have brought the dead out of their coffins had there been any in the neighborhood.

For the second time that night the shrieks of men and neighing of horses arose as the Leopard's company of attackers dispersed, each man for himself. Blight gave Sarah a stick of burning punk and she took over one chute while he distributed the rockets and whistle bombs indiscriminately, as fast as they could be fired. Some of the men fleeing across fields or under trees found themselves pursued by fire or blood-curdling screams and explosions. One dud wobbled in erratic loops dangerously close to the thatched roof of the inn, watched anxiously by the four. But it went out . . . and fell beyond.

Finally, as the lane and fields emptied, the three cannoneer turned their chutes up at steep angles and the remainder of the fireworks went sizzling up into the grey-black sky and burst in showers of rainbow stars. The very last sparkles dropped into darkness, and the cloud of smoke, still hanging in the air, gradually drifted away and dissolved. Then Chase Longshanks came down the lane on foot, leading his horse -- still stepping nervously from the fireworks. He tethered the horse and tapped gently on the inn door. It opened and he went in.

"That was terrific while it lasted," Tarquin said.

"It looked very effective to me," said Sarah. And Blight added, "I don't think the Leopard will ride this way again. Not for a long time."

Crispin stood looking up into the sky, wishing there were just one more burst of fireworks to dazzle his eyes. Instead, the clouds began to loosen and break up, and in one deep blue opening burned a single star.

* * *

Inside The Legendary Boar, Chase, Frederick Riverford, his wife and his mother, were seated around a table on which burned a single candle. Behind them in the shadows stood the young scullery boy, the girl who milked the cows and helped with the housework, and the two stablemen. They had drawn together, deeply disturbed by what seemed to be a cosmic display above them. They had not seen much from the windows of the inn; they had been too frightened to look out. But they had heard the shrieking whistles and the rattle of explosions. They huddled together in the big room downstairs and tried not to think about what might be coming next.

Fear haunted the eyes of Frederick's wife, who whispered, "Can it be the end of the world . . . and . . . the Judgment?"

"Sweetheart, I don't know," her husband said, taking her hand. "It has been awfully quiet since. I'm beginning to think it may have been a little too localized for the Last Day. Or so I hope."

" 'Localized,' yes, that's the word," said Chase. "My first thought as I came along was of the Judgment, too. But now that I think about it, it seems pretty clear that, whatever it was, it was directed to defending the ford, this inn, and nothing else."

"So you can still watch the little one grow up," and Frederick gently squeezed and shook his wife's hand.

"We still don't know what has become of the Abbot and his monks," said Frederick's mother. "Might it be that they had a hand in this?"

"Abbot Blaise is an enormously wise and clever man, Mother. Who knows what he may have discovered in his books?"

Outside the silence continued. The river whispered and chuckled over the ford, and then the breeze, freshening as dawn approached, loosened an autumn leaf or two. Finally Chase got up from the table, went to the door and stepped cautiously outside. Frederick, his wife, and his mother, followed him out. They looked up at the scattering clouds and saw, in an opening of deepest blue, a single star.

"Do you think that's where the abbot went?" asked the young wife.

"Oh my dear," Frederick replied, "I think he's much closer than that."

FIFTEEN

SHARPENING CLAWS

The door into the chamber was opened cautiously from the other side. The Leopard stuck his head through the opening and looked around. "Who's here?" he asked in a sepulchral whisper. Meanwhile, the two real leopards edged passed his legs and came in. Seeing no one and getting no response, the Archduke pushed the door wide open and entered. His cloak was still wet from the rain and the river, his hat was moist and its feather twisted and bedraggled. His boots squelched slightly with each step. He took off his cap and let it drop to the floor and untied his cloak, which he likewise dropped. Then he slowly revolved a full 360 degrees, looking closely into every corner or shadow, with large, fearful eyes.

The comfortable early morning sun shone into the window bays, but the walls of the castle were so tremendously thick that the sunlight had not yet reached into the room. The two cats stepped up into one of the bays, stretched out in the sunlight and promptly fell asleep. Axel, on the other hand, went to the table and rang the silver bell impatiently . . . and waited. Then he clapped his hands together and waited again. Finally he went to the door and shouted, "Ho! Varlets! Is there no one awake in this godforsaken castle?" Realizing how he had just described his home, he again looked fearfully about.

But word of the Archduke's return eventually reached the kitchens and, before too long, he was ordering people about, not with the customary tone of unquestioned authority as formerly, but as a spoiled child who, if he were not obeyed, would weep. They built him a huge fire because he was frozen to the bone. They brought him dry clothes and towels warmed at the fire. They struggled mightily to remove his sodden boots. They brought him a cup full of brandy and a breakfast with chops, a pitcher of spiced, warmed wine, and a whole plate of comfits. They put a sleeveless, velvet gown lined with fur on him and lined slippers also warmed at the fire, pushed his big chair up in front of the fire, handed him the silver bell, picked up his damp clothing and his boots and retired, leaving the door ajar to be sure someone heard the bell should it be rung again.

There he sat, like a painted icon, haggard, white-faced, hollow eyes gazing into the fire. Gradually, very gradually, some little color returned to his face. What with the warmth, what with the food and drink, what with the flickering flames, his eyelids grew heavy and began to close. Then suddenly he let out a hoarse cry and started to his feet. The silver bell dropped to the stones and rang crazily as it rolled in circles, and the leopards sat upright in their bay. Almost instantly a servant appeared, bowing and inquiring, "Your Grace?"

The Archduke eyed him with great suspicion, as though he had never seen him before, and then exclaimed, "Send for Ulf and Dorn! But pick up that bell first!" He stood there with hand and arm stretched out imperiously until the quaking servant handed him the bell and disappeared. He gathered his gown more tightly around him and sat back down. Noticing that the leopards had gone back to their sunny drowse, he commanded, "Come here!" They were not as prompt as the servant, but with animals the Archduke was slightly more patient. He stroked their heads for a bit but shooed them back into their window as Ulf and Dorn appeared.

The two henchmen had also changed their clothes but they too had an expression of deathwatch and despair on their faces. Seeing their condition restored the Leopard's spirits a little, but only a very little. He stood up, went to the table, set down the bell so that it would not ring, said, "Close that door," to Ulf and, "Bring my chair," to Dorn. "Now," seating himself again in his customary place at the head of the table, "what horrible black magic were we afflicted with last night? Was it real, or some dreadful illusion of hell fires?" Once again the memory drained the color from his face, a result lost on the other two.

"Was't no illusion," Dorn said softly, fearful of speaking aloud, "the back of my doublet's nearly scorched through."

"And my cloak is full of little holes, must be a hundred – burns they are," volunteered Ulf.

"You've seen nothing since? We've not been followed by flaming banshees or something worse?"

The memory of the collapsing bridge and the attack of the screaming, fiery devils, was still so terrifying to Dorn and Ulf that they paid no attention to the fear in the eyes of the Archduke. Instead, they looked about uncomfortably and drew closer to the table and their leader in his chair.

"It was the Grey Wolf, the Grey Wolf," their leader was muttering. "I'm sure it must have been. The Grey Wolf of Harklinden, my brother. I never thought, I never dreamed he had such powers in his control." He sat in total frustration, leaning on his elbow and pushing on his clenched teeth with his thumb. Then he demanded pen, ink, and parchment, which they dutifully brought.

For the rest of the morning he alternately sat at the table shredding quill pens or pacing up and down, back and forth, until the leopards were quite beside themselves and had to be taken out of the room. At the top of a large sheet the archduke had scrawled in great black letters, **LIFTING THE BAN**. But after that beginning he stuck fast, discarding idea after idea, plot after plot, as either too easy or utterly impossible. What he wanted was something impossibly possible and that is what he was determined to get.

By mid-afternoon he had wasted several sheets, come close to inventing the parchment glider without ever realizing it (that was when the cats had to be led away), and finally, in angry desperation decided to inspect his castle. He wound a dry cloak about him, seized his riding crop and, with Dorn on one wing and Ulf on the other, set off at a furious pace. Guards in their guardrooms turned pale as they tried to conceal dice and cups of wine and straighten their uniforms; sentries lounging at their posts felt the crop come down on their backs and shoulders; cooks and scullions in the kitchen sent geese and ducks spinning on their spits or dropped ladles into vats of soup in surprise; bakers sent up clouds of flour in the centers of which they tried to conceal themselves; laundresses, at the sight of the flying Archduke swooping down upon them, screamed and threw their aprons over their faces.

Fortunately the hawks and falcons on their perches in the mews were hooded and could not return the glare of their master as he swept through, but the hounds in the kennels sent up a chorus of wailing and howls that alerted the rest of the castle so that in the stables the ostlers and grooms were hard at work on the harness and the smith in his smithy made the sparks fly upward and the white-hot horseshoe ring on the anvil.

Up towers and along wall walks and down towers he went, leaving a wake of distraught faces and nervous hearts behind him until there was no place left to visit but the chapel. So he went there. He had turned the chaplain out years ago as an unnecessary adjunct and had not been there since, although it was adjacent to his suite. Now he strode in and looked around. He stared at the wall painting of Christ on the cross, sniffed arrogantly and said, "Make this the treasury; it's wasted space; it ought to be good for something." Then he smiled wryly and added, "The money may be safer here."

Only twice before during his inspection had he paused long enough for Ulf and Dorn to catch up to him. The first was in the kitchen to demand a taste of the soup. The chief cook with trembling hand had passed him a ladle of soup; he blew on it a few times and then tasted, pronounced it "Execrable" and stalked on. The second time was in the kennels where, despite the yelping and howling, he came to a full stop before the wolfhounds and regarded them intently. "Have them ready tomorrow for the hunt," said the Leopard of Tryce.

At night the Leopard ate in the great hall, usually a sign of high festivity. Not that night. He sat slumped in the high chair, picking at the food and waving away dish after dish. He scowled from under his brows at anybody and everybody who dared to look or sound the least bit cheerful. He fiddled with his knife and twiddled his wine cup, then sent word to the musicians in the gallery to play something cheerful and when they did pounded the table and shouted, "Not that, fools!" Eventually he stood up (everyone else jumped to their feet) and stormed out calling for "Lights, lights!"

Servants brought candles to his room. He sent them back for more, but still there were dark corners or shadowy places so he sent them away for more and more. Before long not a flat surface in the room but was covered with candles and rush lights. Even the floor was filled with flames so that one could scarcely navigate the room without getting his shins singed. Then the windows had to be set ajar to let the smoke out, which only made things worse as the candles guttered and the flames leapt until the entire room seemed to dance and shake. The Leopard paid no heed; he scratched and scrawled, crossed out and blotted, sent out for more ink and quills, and fell-to again until his fingers grew black with ink and his eyes were rimmed with ink where he had tried to dig the sleep out of the corners.

Then he was finished. Haggard, with blackened, hollow eyes, he gathered his parchment into a stack, weighed them down with the silver bell, and went to bed. Even the lights he left behind, all but a few.

The next day, in the clarity of late October, the Archduke of Tryce and a considerable entourage of huntsmen and hounds rode into the forest to hunt for wolves.

SIXTEEN

THE LEOPARD IN DECEMBER

"There's a rider crossing the ford!"

The Guardian looked up from where he was going over accounts with a merchant of wines and spirits. "Alone?" he asked.

"Yes. Far as eye can see," from the ostler who had opened the door and leaned in to announce the rider.

"Anyone we know?"

"If I had to guess," said the ostler, "I'd say it was the Leopard of Tryce."

"No retinue . . . escort . . . no hoodlums?"

The ostler looked out again. "Not unless they're well back in the forest."

Riverford stood up. "Excuse me," he said to the merchant. "I hope not to be long." The merchant shrugged and made an expansive gesture. He acknowledged that he was not quite at the top of the priority scale at The Legendary Boar. He hoisted himself to his feet and eased out the door behind the Guardian, over-come by curiosity.

The bright sunlight had not yet begun to melt last night's dusting of early December snow, and the brightness made both men wrinkle their noses and squint as their eyes watered. The Guardian had to raise an arm against the sun, still in the east, so that he could take a look at the rider approaching.

It was the Leopard all right, but not on Backlash. Instead, he was riding a cheerful-looking mare of no particular distinction. Regardless of his mount, the Archduke had dressed himself splendidly in fur-lined garments, his heavy golden chain of office around his neck and a clip of gold and diamonds flashed where it held the feathers to his bonnet. Behind his saddle was tied a large, wicker hamper over which had been tied a rolled up leopard skin, the fur side in.

"Riverford," the Archduke said, swinging down from his horse and extending his hand, "I come as a penitent seeking peace."

The Guardian took the hand that was offered and shook it without much enthusiasm, in fact, with some reluctance. He said nothing in reply.

"Understandably, you proceed with caution," continued the other," but your caution is unnecessary. A lesson learned is wisdom gained. I stand here a wiser man, ready to mend fences and to confirm you as Guardian of the Ford, if that is at all helpful." Without waiting for a reply, he turned cheerfully to the merchant. "And good morning to you, Bo Tunstall. I am happy to see that you have more customers than just those in Tryceholdings. Drop in on my steward soon; he will have an order prepared."

"Thank you, your grace," said Bo Tunstall, making a leg and a bow that knew where the butter went.

In his bonnet with its long pheasant feathers and the rest of his slightly overpowering outfit, the resemblance between the Archduke and the Guardian of the Ford was not nearly so apparent. At least not to Bo Tunstall. Shortly thereafter the three went into the inn, where the shadows were heavier. The merchant, sensing that the Archduke had something of a private nature to transact, did the prudent thing. He mounted and rode away.

Meanwhile, Axel exerted all his charm, which, when he put his mind to it, was considerable. By the time he had left he had put into the hands of Frederick Riverford a small iron casket of impregnable design and the key that went with it. Inside the casket was the Ring of Harklinden on a golden chain. He asked Riverford to keep the casket safe for the one who would come along to lift the ban on abbey and forest. "Guard it as you do the ford," he said, meaning to compliment. He also presented the host with the leopard skin, to be used in place of a saddle blanket – "A friendly memento from me," the Leopard smiled. More likely a *memento mori*, Riverford thought privately. But he accepted the two gold coins to be used for replacements when the original skin wore out. To the host it seemed impolite and small-minded to refuse. Crispin, had he been there, would have recognized the Leopard's performance for what it was, but appreciated its quality. The Guardian suspected that he was being used but could not quite decipher how it was working, or to what end.

"And a boar's head," cried the Archduke, as though the thought had just struck him. "You have no boar's head except the one on the sign. I will send you a truly legendary stuffed head from Tryceholdings Guard. For over the hearth," he gestured to the enormous fireplace around which the little inn had been built. "An inn with such a name deserves a fitting figurehead." He left shortly thereafter, once again shaking Riverford's hand. Finally, he leaned down from the saddle and said quietly, "There's no reason why we two should be enemies. *Especially* we two."

"Well, he certainly understands my parentage," the Guardian reported back inside.

"Can he possibly be up to any good?"

"I don't know, Mother, and I wonder whether we'll ever find out. But surely the Ring is intended for whoever succeeds in lifting the Ban. Whoever that turns out to be, he will be perfectly obvious to us, at least according to the Leopard, who is, I believe, heading for Longshanks Hall."

The Leopard smiled to himself as he jogged along, quite pleased with his work thus far.

* * *

Chase was about to ride out on a cob with a couple of hounds to try to locate a fox den. He was just in time to see Axel coming over the rim of the bowl, brilliantly dressed even against the snow. He trotted around to head him off before he reached the great door but was too late. The Leopard had already dismounted and was about to raise the knocker as he came up. The hounds started to bark until silenced by a word from their master.

"Ah, Chase, there you are," said Axel smoothly. "I was about to inquire after you."

"And here I am, conveniently enough." He did not bother to dismount. Instead he looked silently down on the Archduke where he stood, rich in his finery of damask and fur. The Leopard had been rehearsing his next speech for some time. He thought he could get through it without giving himself away so he unleashed it now.

"I made a terrible mistake when I attacked you several weeks ago. It was only as I was riding home, wet and miserable, that I realized what a friend I had lost. And lost through my own fault, through my own jealousy and temper, through my own selfishness and pride. Perhaps, had my father not welcomed me back like the Prodigal Son after I had lost Trycemeadows, I might have learned my lesson earlier. But before this younger son could collect his wits my father was gone, my brother Blaise had surrendered everything and gone off to become the Abbot of Harklinden, and I was the new Archduke, able to do just about anything I pleased. So the lesson took time to learn. Nevertheless, learn it I did, and that is what brings me to Longshanks Hall and to you, Chase, to extend my hand as a friend asking forgiveness of a friend."

Chase dismounted immediately. He figured it was the least he could do. Even he was surprised that Axel had said what he had said without gagging. *But then*, he thought, *he never lacked daring. Courage maybe, but not daring.* "What is it that you want?" he asked. He deliberately kept his hands occupied with reins and saddle, pointedly ignoring the other man's outstretched hand, until he shrugged and lowered it. Chase felt that once he accepted the other's hand he would be committed to going forward into something unknown that he might bitterly regret. But the Leopard had foreseen this development and was not unprepared.

"I understand why you refuse to grasp the hand of friendship when it is offered, but I am saddened as well. You were always a generous man, Chase, bold, fearless, an example to us all. I am grieved that, now that I have changed, I find that you have changed too."

"Your brother and his monks have disappeared, God knows where; the Abbey of Harklinden and its entire forest lies under ban, *your* ban. For the second time, what is it that you want?"

"I need your help."

"What for?"

The Archduke looked about him and made a gesture which indicated that he would prefer to talk elsewhere, privately.

"Axel, I am not going to invite you inside. Anything you have to say to me can be said here as well as anywhere else."

The other raised his eyebrows but smiled, somewhat ruefully. "You are a hard man, Chase," he said.

"No. I am not. But careful? Yes, I *am* careful."

"Careful, then. All right. I need you to help me prepare for the lifting of the ban on Harklinden."

"What have you to do with that?"

"The terms for lifting the ban have been left to my discretion. You see this hamper here?" He nodded to the hamper tied up behind his saddle. "It contains bread and wine, a chalice, plate, and a fine linen cloth – symbolical gifts. Sometime after my death there will come one in quest of this hamper. You are to surrender it to him when he asks for it."

"It seems an unnecessarily long time to wait. How am I to recognize him?"

"He will be only seven years old."

Then Chase saw clearly that he was facing the Leopard of Tryce, the same unrepentant, rapacious Axel that he knew. "Suppose I refuse?" he asked.

"My dear Chase, it is all quite simple; the decision is entirely yours. Should you refuse, the ban will never be lifted."

There had been no change, only a new plan, more devious than the attack, a plan that would bind Chase and perhaps his heirs for years and years. There was nothing that he could do, so he agreed.

Then the Leopard smiled broadly and said, "Perhaps 'Longshanks' was worth losing after all."

SEVENTEEN

TAKING THE LONG WAY HOME

"Herkimer, Barton, Plymouth, and West. Good morning. . . . No, I am sorry, Mr. West is still in conference. May I take a message? . . . You would like to speak with Sarah Falkrest as soon as the conference is over. And your name is? Crispin Agincroft, of course. Has she your phone number? . . . West Waffle 619. I will be sure to tell her. You're welcome. Goodbye."

Crispin put the receiver back in its cradle and looked up at his mother.

"You did very well," she said. "That's all there is to it. Now unwind your legs from that chair."

It had been the boy's first telephone call. He had thought his mother would make it for him and had been appalled when she said he was getting old enough to make it himself. So he had got out the phone book and looked up the number of the law offices of Herkimer, Barton, Plymouth, and West. He dialed the local operator, gave Mrs. Verax the number and waited until she said, "Go ahead, please." Mrs. Verax knew everybody's business in the West Waffle Exchange, although she always denied knowing anything.

By the time he was through, tiny beads of perspiration had broken out across his forehead and he had wound his own legs around the legs of the chair. He felt as though he had thrown up an elephant. But his mother did not have to prompt him to say "Thank you," a big point in his favor. Now all he had to do was wait for the phone to ring.

His mother regarded him with kindly amusement. "A watched pot never boils," she said, "and a phone never rings while you wait. Why don't you teach Justin how to catch his ball out on the lawn? I have to go over accounts with Henriette. I'll answer the phone when it rings and call you."

Colonel Falkrest, Sarah, Mrs. Presskit and the ledger had all gone off to the lawyers that morning to make sure of the legal ground under their feet before approaching the bankers. Mrs. Presskit had discovered that Mrs. Falkrest, before she died, and unbeknownst to her husband, had monthly been skimming off as much money as she dared and putting it into a numbered account for a 'rainy day.' She had been doing this from the day she was married, as had her mother and grandmother before her. It seems to have been a tradition of the Longshanks women, born as a result of the initial burden of debt. Mrs. Falkrest was descended from those women. Estate agents and accountants had been sworn to secrecy. They well understood the necessity of the oath. Now that Colonel Falkrest was struggling so hard to keep the estate intact for Sarah, he wanted to tap into that account to take some of the pressure off. More importantly, he wanted to take his daughter to some place that would work to strengthen her legs and put her back on her feet. The account was so fixed that all withdrawals had to be countersigned by a female descendant in the direct line. Sarah had noticed the odd monthly inserts in the ledgers she had gone through but, since they were so regular and since everything had been signed and countersigned by her mother or her grandmother, and so forth, she had concluded that it must have something to do with taxes.

Crispin, Sarah, and Tarquin had all squeezed together under the umbrella after the fracas at the ford, and all three had been taken at once, leaving Blight for a solo flight with the launching chutes. They had not been back in the library too long, gloating (it must be admitted) over their success in routing the Leopard and his minions, when the Colonel, Mrs. Presskit and the ledger, marched in to confirm what that lady had already indicated to Sarah.

"Oh Dads," the girl said, "I don't think we should cross our bridges before they hatch . . . or count our . . . oh, never mind. You know what I mean. I don't think we should."

"You are right, as you always are (almost)." He gave his daughter an enveloping hug which practically dragged her from her wheelchair. Then he shook hands with Blight, Tarquin, and Crispin, too. Finally he gave an astonished Mrs. Presskit a kiss on both cheeks. "We already have an appointment with Ben West for the day after tomorrow. D'you know, his office is in one of the only buildings in Tryceholdings with an elevator? Otherwise we would have to ask them to drive out here because, Zascha, you are essential at the powow."

So it came about that Sarah in her wheelchair, her father, and Mrs. Presskit and the ledger, all squeezed into an elevator (that appeared more like a birdcage than anything), while it wheezed its way up nine floors to the offices of the lawyers.

* * *

The phone rang. Mrs. Agincroft called her son. He hurried in the shortest way – through the windows into the dining room and into the hall – and took the receiver from his mother as she said, "Here he is," and handed it to him.

"Hello, Sarah? How did everything go?"

"It's to be Badfensterbad, if the bankers agree."

"It's too what?" All the b's had confused Crispin.

"Badfensterbad. It's the place Dads is going to take me. It's a spa with hot springs and husky women to punch me up and flatten me out and generally make me over, I guess."

"Holy casmittima! And everything is all legal and everything?"

"Yes, so it would seem. Dads is still pumping everybody's hands and pounding them on the back; Mrs. Presskit is beaming like Christmas and may never let go of that ledger."

"I would have liked to have been there."

"I know you would, but much of it was pretty boring and difficult to follow. My attention would wander and then they'd have to explain bits again until I understood. But we all agreed at the end. Can you ask your mother if it's all right if we stop by? Dads thinks I haven't been out of Longshanks for so long that he wants to take the long way home and stop off for a minute or two at your place. Would that be all right?"

"Hold on. I'll ask." He did. It was. And so they came, although Mrs. Presskit had finally relinquished the ledger and gone back to the office of Presskit and Kuntz, Auctioneers.

Mrs. Agincroft and Henriette shifted gears and Sarah and the Colonel stayed for dinner. Tarquin, who was sitting next to the girl and across from her father, covered himself with glory. He plied both with questions and told amusing anecdotes to such a degree that his mother raised an eyebrow at her husband, a sign Crispin happened to catch. Mr. Agincroft looked back at his wife with a completely expressionless face but with both eyes sparkling.

The Falkrest duo left soon after dinner so that they would not miss the last ferry at Wider Water. While the Colonel and his father were gerrymandering the wheelchair into the back seat of the car, Crispin stepped up onto the running board next to Sarah. "Who will McGuiness have to bully while you're away?" he asked.

"I don't know. Nobody, I guess. He's afraid of the Silent Woman and there won't be anybody else in the house. Do you suppose you could go over once in a while and give him tit for tat? If he has no one to practice on he might go soft. But you have to give back as good as you get, otherwise he will be impossible."

The boy promised that he would. "I'll try to get Tarquin to go along; he doesn't let anyone push him around."

"No, no. You have to let Mac win a few, too. The trick is to keep it about even and then you'll both be happy. I'm not sure Tarquin can do that."

So they said "Goodbye" and Crispin stepped back down off the running board. At once, he noticed for the first time that, for a boy who was almost eight, the running board was not as high as it had been.

THE END

Made in the USA
Charleston, SC
08 June 2013